KNIGHT SIR LOUIS

AND THE
SINISTER SNOWBALL

**GUPPY
BOOKS**

Papers used by Guppy Books are from well-managed
forests and other responsible sources.

GUPPY PUBLISHING LTD Reg. No. 11565833

A CIP catalogue record for this book is
available from the British Library.

Typeset in 13½/20 pt Adobe Garamond by
Falcon Oast Graphic Art Ltd, www.falcon.uk.com

Printed and bound in Great Britain by CPI Books Ltd

Hip 'ip ... s fo e ... ouis ...

'Absolutely h... rious non... se. I even forgive them for spelling my name wrong in the title, that's how funny it is.' Louie Stowell

'Sublimely funny and seriously entertaining, this is the ideal way to get your youngsters hooked on reading. . . and medieval mischief!'
Lancashire Evening Post

'What a hero! What a story! Sublime daftness on every page.'
Jeremy Strong

'I love these books so much! *Mr Gum* levels of weird and brilliant'
Jo Nadin

"Probably the funniest book I've ever read. A masterclass in silliness!"
Gary Northfield, author of *Julius Zebra* series

'A ridiculously appealing story . . . wacky, original, fantastic and funny, it's so good you'll have to read it for yourself!' *School Librarian*

'Brimming with ludicrous magic and fizzing with irresistible comedy.'
Peter Lord

'As if Hans Christian Andersen had cornered you in a pub and got his own yarn in the wrong order, or The Brothers Grimm had squeezed up next to you with a Tupperware box of home-made sandwiches on a long
c...

'D...

'Will appeal to any who likes adventures and laughing.'
Philip Reeve

'One of the funniest books you will read this year!' – My Book Corner

'Refreshing and entertaining.' – Books for Topics

'This book made me feel happy and I want to read more in this series – a 5 ☆ book' *Rubiroo, aged 9*

'These books are stone cold smashers!'
Stuart Heritage

'I was laughing at lots of parts in this book!'
Ibrahim, aged 9

'My 9-year-old boy loved it and I could hear him chuckling to himself while he was engrossed in the book.'
A Wilford

'I loved this book as it was LAUGH OUT LOUD!' Bweemz, aged 10

'My son could not literally put this down. You don't get many books with belly laughs and giggles but this hit the spot for my almost-7-year-old.' Chris Lee

'I think the Brothers McLeod are really good at telling stories because Knight Sir Louis is funny in so many unimaginable ways.' **Annabel, aged 9**

To Louis, Lyla, Audrey, Finty and Rosa

So WHO's IN THIS

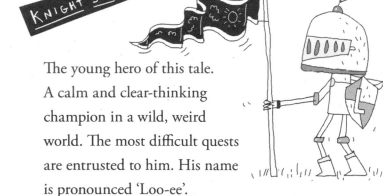

The young hero of this tale.
A calm and clear-thinking
champion in a wild, weird
world. The most difficult quests
are entrusted to him. His name
is pronounced 'Loo-ee'.

CLUNKALOT

A trusty (never rusty) robot horse. Sturdy, brave and
always ready to join Louis on a dangerous quest. Also
loves flying and poetry.

BOOK EXACTLY?

HENRIETTA CATALOGUE

A super-smart boar with a love of adventure, mushrooms and adventure. Did I mention she likes adventure? And mushrooms.

PEARLIN

A young, self-taught wizentor (that's a wizard *and* inventor). Always coming up with new and fun ways to use machines and magic.

KING BURT THE NOT BAD

The (mostly) kind and often (not) sensible King of Squirrel Helm who rules from Castle Sideways.

DAVE THE SWORD

A magical sword recycled from a magic mirror. Likes reflecting magical spells, chopping through nasty things, and singing. (Is an awful singer).

CHAMPION TRIXIE

A wise, no-nonsense, champion knight. Also . . . she's Knight Sir Louis' mum.

SIR TYMUR TRAFELA

Headmaster at the Knights of the Future School (KOFS for short).

SIR YUKI

A daring young knight with a very loud voice. DRAGONFLAP, HO!

CRAYKO LE FAUX

A cunning knight. An expert cheat. Usually seen with his pet bird Peck.

SPLINT

Supreme Overlord of the freezing cold Brrrrrland.

Splint's five little siblings and helpers.

THE FIVE SNOWBALLS

CHAPTER 1
BELOW ZERO

Welcome to Castle Sideways in the Kingdom of Squirrel Helm!

Squirrel Helm has four seasons.

SPRING

SUMMER

AUTUMN

WINTER

Now, let's head further north to the country of Brrrrland.

Brrrrland also has four seasons.

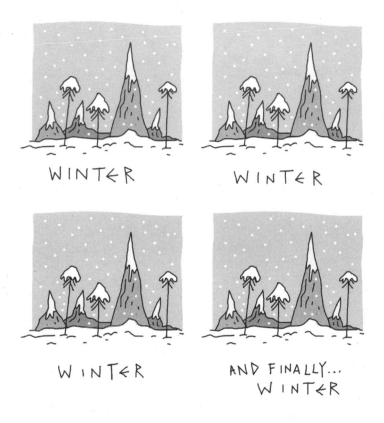

WINTER

WINTER

WINTER

AND FINALLY...
WINTER

Except for one year when a weather wizard stopped by. Then there was:

Winter.

Winter.

Winter.

And a new season, Roo-bee-doo-dang.

During Roo-bee-doo-dang all the snow turned orange and tasted of pineapple. It also snowed upwards.

CHAPTER ZERO

They say Brrrrland is home to lots of different icy creatures, including . . .

ICE GOLEMS

ICICLE TOOTHED WALRUSES

SSSSSSS_{ssss}

SNOW SNAKES

BLIZZARD CROCODILES

AN ICE CHICKEN CALLED BRENDA

THE MICRO YETI

A MENKVEE

A HANDFUL OF SNOWBALLS

Do these things really exist? Well . . . I don't know. But I'm sure we'll find out.

We'll be spending quite a bit of time in the land of Brrrrrland so you might want to find a warm hat and some toasty gloves. You don't want to catch a cold from this book. Brrrr. But for now, let's head to the warmth of Chapter One.

CHAPTER 1

It was dinner time at Castle Sideways. Dinner was always tasty, but these days it wasn't very surprising. Not since King Burt had rediscovered his favourite childhood meal.

CASTLE SIDEWAYS FOOD PLANNER

THIS WEEK AND EVERY WEEK

MONDAY
BEANS ON TOAST.

TUESDAY
TOAST WITH BEANS

8

WEDNESDAY
BEANS WITH TOAST ON THE SIDE.

THURSDAY
BEANS ON HOT BREAD

FRIDAY
FISH (MADE FROM BEANS) AND CHIPS (MADE FROM TOAST)

SATURDAY
BEAN SANDWICH (TOASTED)

SUNDAY
ROAST BEANS AND TOAST POTATOES

Knight Sir Louis, champion knight at Castle Sideways, was completely fed up with beans. So he decided to see if he could make some changes.

On his travels he had met an ogre called Dollop. Dollop was a wonderful chef and Louis asked him to visit and to cook for everyone at Castle Sideways.

'But does he know how to cook beans on toast?'
asked King Burt. 'I do like beans on toast. And
toast and beans.'

'Yes, your majesty, we'd noticed,' said Louis soothingly, 'but Dollop can cook anything.'

'Then tonight we will feast on beany toasties!' said Burt.

'I was thinking we could try something called pizza,' said Louis.

'Does it have beans on it?' asked King Burt.

'Not usually,' said Louis.

WHAT'S YOUR FAVE PIZZA TOPPING?
CUSTARD
WHAT?
TRY IT. TASTES LOVELY.

It turned out that King Burt did like pizza. King Burt asked Dollop to stay and appointed him Head Chef to Castle Sideways. Everyone was relieved. Everyone except Farmer Pinto who supplied the castle with tins of beans.

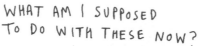

WHAT AM I SUPPOSED TO DO WITH THESE NOW?

One pizza night during the month of Yoghurt, Louis was sitting beside his friends Pearlin the wizentor and Henrietta Catalogue the talking boar.

'Oo! My pizza has lovely truffling mushrooms,' said Catalogue happily.

'I'm well hungry,' said Pearlin, wide-eyed with pleasure. 'I didn't have lunch cos my pet dragon ate it.'

'I suppose that's what you get if your pet dragon has two heads!' laughed Louis.

MAC

CHEESE

12

Before they tucked in, King Burt stood and made an announcement.

'My good subjects, here we are once more enjoying delicious food. Thank you, Dollop. And thank you, Sir Louis, for showing me that there was more to dinner than beans on toast.'

'In fact,' continued the king, 'I've realised I've become stuck in my ways. It's time to do things differently. To think OUTSIDE THE BOX!'

'Sounds good,' said Pearlin, who was always creating new magical inventions.

'Sounds fun times,' said Catalogue, who loved discovering weird new plants.

'Sounds amazing,' said Louis, who loved unexpected adventures.

'And that is why . . .' continued King Burt, '. . . I am sending Knight Sir Louis to school!'

The room went very quiet.

CHAPTER 2

'You're sending me to school?' said Louis to King Burt.

'That's right!' answered Burt.

'But why?' said Louis, panicking.

'Because I'm doing things differently!' said King Burt. 'And also because, by total coincidence, I just received this amazing letter from a school.'

He waved a letter about in the air. It seemed to glow around the edges and made little swooshing bleeps as it moved about.

'But where? Which school?' said Louis.

'Oh. Somewhere called School for Knights of the Future, or Future Knight School, or something like that. Anyway, it's called KOFS, for short.'

'KOFS! For how long?' said Louis.

'Oh, I don't know. A few weeks. Months maybe. Years. Do you know, I'm not really sure,' said the king.

Louis was stunned. He'd never been to school. Growing up, he'd taken lessons with his mother, Champion Trixie. She'd taught all the important subjects . . .

'But what if I don't want to go?' said Louis.

'Are you a king?' asked King Burt calmly.

'No,' said Louis. (Though he had once been a king for about a day.)

'He is a deputy king!' pointed out Pearlin.

IS THAT AS IMPORTANT AS AN ACTUAL KING?

'Suppose not,' said Pearlin.

'Then Louis should do what his king says,' explained Burt. 'And I am that king and, now that I'm *thinking differently,* I say he's going to school. End of chat. Over and out. Full stop. The end.'

And he handed over a fat envelope to Louis before heading off to play on his latest computer game.

After he'd gone, Pearlin said, 'Sometimes I think we should be able to vote for kings and queens. Then when they do stuff like sending you to school, you could unvote them and tell them to clear off.'

'I like a bit of schooling,' said Catalogue, who sometimes taught at the famous Hogford University. 'I like finding out new things. Maybe you'll enjoy it?'

'I don't know,' said Louis anxiously. 'I like adventures with dragons and battles with evil wizards. I'm not sure that'll be on the school timetable.'

'Bound to be,' said Catalogue. 'It's a school for knights, ain't it?'

CHAPTER 3

Louis was going to school. He let out a big sigh. But that didn't really help. So instead, he decided to let his feelings out in a different way.

AGHHHHH!
THIS ISN'T FAIR!

Louis looked at the envelope from the knights' school. He sliced it open with his magic sword Dave and read it to Pearlin and Catalogue. There were some bits crossed out, but he could just about read those too.

NON FRIGDUS FUTURUM
OBEYUS AN' STUDIHEER

From the Headteacher
Professor Sir Tymur Trafela

Dearest Knight Sir Louis,

We very much look forward to welcoming you to our school, the Knights of the Future School (KOFS). ~~We need to train you to save~~

~~the whole world from becoming a freezing wasteland.~~ We would like you to come here pretty-please with a cherry on top. Please please please please please!!!

We are a boarding school, so you will be sleeping here during term time. If you would like to send messages home you can use our ~~powerful super-computer from the future~~ old-fashioned telephone. If you prefer the really old ways, you can use one of our owls to send a message.

To be honest, I wouldn't bother, the owls usually just tear the letters to shreds and make nests out of them. But it's up to you.

Please do arrive on time!

Toewig

TIME is very important.

There is no TIME to waste. TIME waits for no one. Please please please arrive by dawn, the last Moonday of the Month of Yoghurt. If you arrive late, ~~you will be helping to doom the planet to an everlasting winter~~ it will be quite annoying.

Yours ~~in total desperation~~ from the perfectly calm,

Sir Tymur Trafela

Professor Sir Tymur Trafela

Address: you will find the school near the top of volcano Mount Badaboom.

'Funny letter,' commented Catalogue. 'Kind of nice but those crossed-out bits are a bit oodle-poodle.'

'You'd better get moving,' said Pearlin. 'Dawn, last Moonday of the Month of Yoghurt. That's tomorrow morning!'

Louis had noticed that too. He didn't have long to get ready. But there was no way that he was going to school without two things . . .

1. His magic sword Dave (full name Senator Jibber Jabber Ticket Flick It Sprocket Wicket Dingle David)

2. His trusty steed, the robot horse, Clunkalot!

CHAPTER 4

Let's talk some more about Brrrrland.

Did you know that most people don't believe Brrrrland exists?

HANDS UP WHO THINKS BRRRRRLAND IS JUST A MADE-UP PLACE?

There was a nasty blizzard blowing down from Brrrrland. This was not normal. Storms usually

stayed in Brrrrrland, circling around and around. But this one was different. It rushed over the tall mountains that stood like a pointy crown around Brrrrrland. This storm was going on an adventure.

It rushed down to a little village called Last Hopeton and froze it solid. It rushed onwards to a slightly larger village called Almost End and froze that solid too. A few hours later, it was still going strong. It reached a small city called Coldington Splip.

The whole town was out for their spring celebration. Any minute, the winter was due to end and the flowers would begin to pop out. But no! Instead of the spring, the freezing cold blizzard brought fresh snow. The mayor was not impressed!

Before the mayor ran back inside his house, he noticed something very strange about the oncoming blizzard. Here and there the storm seemed to have little faces.

Faces with devious, crystal blue eyes and sharp, bright-white teeth set in crafty, smiling mouths. The whole thing was really, quite unpleasant . . .

CHAPTER 5

'We have a problem,' said Pearlin.

This was true. Louis had just a few hours to get to the Knights of the Future School on Mount Badaboom. He was planning to fly on Clunkalot at top speed. But Clunkie wasn't going anywhere.

'Clunkie's getting a new upgrade,' explained Pearlin. 'After it's done, he'll have a new mode. Stinky Skunk Mode. He'll be able to eject a highly stinky stink bomb.'

'Where from?' asked Louis.

'Where do you think?' said Pearlin, pointing at the tail end. Then she patted Clunkie and said sadly, 'If I'd known you needed him for school, I wouldn't have bothered. But he's going to be plugged in for at least another day.'

'Then I'm going to be late!' said Louis, worried. 'Unless . . . why don't I fly there on Mac n Cheese?'

BI – DRAGON

SUPER-HEATED STOMACH

But Mac n Cheese had just left for a camping trip with the Squirrel Helm Scout troop.

SCOUT TRIP.

ON COLD NIGHTS,
KEEP WARM BY
GATHERING AROUND
A FRIENDLY DRAGON.

'So, no Mac n Cheese either!' said Louis, frustrated. 'Is there some other way of getting there? Have you invented a teleportation pill?'

'Nah,' said Pearlin. 'Teleportation magic is pretty weird. Does its own thing. Every time I try it, I get covered in fruit jelly. Don't know what that's about!'

Louis looked around the room for inspiration. There was a pile of Pearlin's inventions in one corner.

'What's this over here?' he asked, pointing at a tennis racket attached to a long wooden arm.

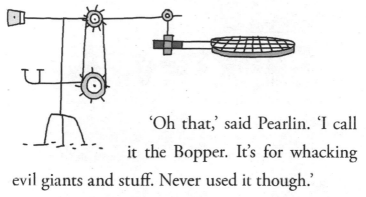

'Oh that,' said Pearlin. 'I call it the Bopper. It's for whacking evil giants and stuff. Never used it though.'

'Do you think it could bop me? Through the sky. BOP! Towards the school?'

'Ooo! Nice! We'd have to set it up just right,' said Pearlin, 'otherwise we might bop you anywhere . . . BOING into the Sea of Sausages, SPLOCK onto the Jabby Mountains, or even WAHOO right off the planet!'

'Well, let's get to work,' said Louis. 'I need to get to school on time, by order of the king. And I've got a tennis racket to catch!'

CHAPTER 6

Even though he was very busy, Louis found a moment to write a letter to his mum with his new address. At that moment, his parents were on holiday in a village called Hardly Here in the northern country of Plopp.

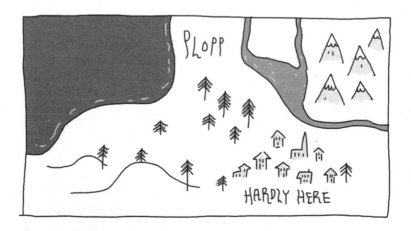

There was no internet or telephone or shops selling plastic knick-knacks. Louis' mum and dad liked it that way. Life was more relaxed. Life was slower. People took their time.

But Louis' letter would never arrive at his parents' holiday cottage, because something strange was about to happen . . .

Trixie was up early practising her pole vaulting. She was still head of her local Guild of Knights and liked to stay in shape in case there was an attack from dragons, wizards or even hostile trolls. Louis' father Ned was also up early checking the henhouse for eggs.

Trixie did a long run-up and thrust down the pole into the ground. She launched herself over the cottage in a graceful arc. But while in the air, she felt a strange breeze. A cold breeze. Suddenly, ice formed all

over her knight's armour. She became as heavy as a stone and plummeted down onto the farmhouse roof . . .

CLONK!

. . . rolled like a snowball off the tiles and landed SPLAT in the mud beside Ned and the chicken hut.

'You all right, my love?' asked Ned, worried.

'Just about,' replied Trixie, picking herself up and knocking chunks of ice from her armour. 'But there's something strange in the air.'

'There's something strange on the ground too,' added Ned, pointing at the chickens.

Trixie looked. Ned was right. Each chicken was encased in a layer of clear ice, as though they were stuck inside glass sculptures. And across the mud, tiny icicles were forming, and spreading. Then the

wind picked up from the north. A blizzard was coming.

'A blizzard? Here? In the month of Yoghurt?' said Ned, confused. 'What's going on?'

'Inside!' shouted Trixie, and they both ran into the farmhouse.

The Brrrrrland blizzard was still going strong. It hit the farmhouse and carried on its journey south. As Louis' mum looked out of the window, she thought she saw five gnashing faces in the storm, each with pointy teeth and bright glinting eyes.

DUN DUN
DURRRRRRR

CHAPTER BADDY

Well now, Chapter Six was very dramatic. And I don't know about you, but I think it's high time we met the baddy of this book.

I'M EXCITED ABOUT THIS.

I WONDER WHO IT COULD BE?

A BIG SURPRISE TO US ALL, I'M SURE.

If the Knight Sir Louis stories were a set of trading cards instead of a set of books then Splint's card would look like this:

SPLINT

SINISTER SNOWBALL

Splint is a giant snowball with a heart of purest ice. Legend says he cannot be melted by anything... not even by red hot chillies collected from the slopes of volcanoes like Mount Badaboom. Splint has ruled for over a hundred years.

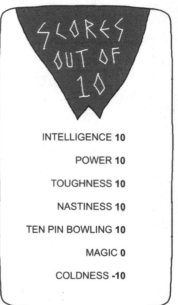

SCORES OUT OF 10

INTELLIGENCE **10**

POWER **10**

TOUGHNESS **10**

NASTINESS **10**

TEN PIN BOWLING **10**

MAGIC **0**

COLDNESS **-10**

Hmm.

A zero for magic. That's interesting. Splint isn't magical. But somehow no wizard, no witch, no sorcerer has ever managed to defeat Splint.

And *hmm.*

Another interesting fact. Splint has five loyal siblings. They are also snowballs, but much smaller. Their names are Flint, Mint, Hint, Clint and Sharon.

Well. There you go. That's the baddy and his little baddy friends. Probably has something to do with that blizzard from the north. Don't you think?

Hmm.

CHAPTER CRUNCH

Splint the Sinister Snowball liked giving instructions. But he didn't want to organise things himself. That was beneath him. So he had a sidekick to do that sort of stuff.

The last thing Splint wanted was a clever sidekick. What if they were so smart they overthrew him? Then he wouldn't be supreme overlord anymore. That's why he'd chosen Crunch to be his Prime Minister.

Knight Sir Louis had been on many missions and for some reason they always seemed to include vegetables. He'd faced down magical potatoes, hunted for ice cucumbers and added corn-on-the-cob to a magical recipe. Little did he know, this adventure was no different. Because Prime Minister Crunch was an evil carrot.

CRUNCH

EVIL CARROT

PRIME MINISTER OF BRRRRRLAND

Crunch is a Prime Minister and a carrot. She has a Masters Degree in Idiotics.

SCORES OUT OF 10

INTELLIGENCE -4

POWER 1

TOUGHNESS 5

NASTINESS 7

TEN PIN BOWLING 0

MAGIC 0

COLDNESS -1

CHAPTER 7

Back at Castle Sideways, Knight Sir Louis was preparing for his first day at school.

READY?

READY!

King Burt was very excited and asked if he could do the countdown.

'Yeah. Go for it, your majesty,' said Pearlin.

'Here we go, then!' said Burt.

TEN, NINE, EIGHT, THREE, SIX, FOUR AND A HALF, TWO, THIRTY FOUR, SIX HUNDRED AND SEVENTY TWO, THREE AGAIN.

Louis decided to speed things up. He lifted up his sword Dave, posing like the hero he was, and interrupted by quickly saying, '*Threetwoone, GO!*'

Pearlin pulled a lever and there was a tremendous WHIRR-WHIRR-WHIRR-WHIRR sound followed by a massive SPROING! The racket swished faster than a lightning bolt strikes and Louis was thrown high into the sky.

'SEE YOU IN THE SCHOOL HOLIDAYS!' he shouted.

A moment later, he was a just a speck in the sky, far away.

Another moment later, and they couldn't see him at all.

Catalogue sighed sadly, 'I'm going to miss Louis, and that's a fact-o.'

Pearlin patted the Bopper. 'Yeah, me too. Glad this worked out though. To be honest, I thought it was a useless pile of junk.'

They looked over at King Burt to see what he'd say; perhaps a comment about how he would miss Louis as well? But he was still busy counting.

EIGHT, SEVEN, SIX, THIRTEEN, TWIFTY, NINETY BORGLE, WINDY FOO, BURKLE, NIMBO-NEE, FLIBBLE, WORRINGTON FUNGE, TWO, FIVE AND THREE QUARTERS.

CHAPTER 8

Louis soared through the air at high speed. It was quite exciting for Louis, but quite confusing for others . . .

OO! IT'S A
KNIGHT FLIGHT!

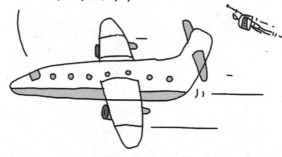

As Louis flew, he began to hear something horrible. He realised it must be his sword, Dave. When the wind whipped across his blade, Dave would sing. But he was an awful singer. No one liked to hear Dave's songs. No one except walruses. They loved his cranky tunes. Sadly, there were no walruses in mid-air to enjoy Dave's song this time.

Perhaps one day walruses will invent the aeroplane. Then they'll be in for a treat.

Louis trusted that Pearlin had correctly calculated his trip. He flew in a perfect arc all the way from Castle Sideways to the school. Flying super-fast up into the air was thrilling. But what comes up, must come down. Flying super-fast down towards the school on the volcano of Mount Badaboom was also thrilling . . . but not in a good way. The ground approached very fast. Fortunately, Pearlin had planned for this.

Louis reached to his shoulder and pulled on the cord. Of course, Louis expected his parachute to open. Instead, it uncorked a magic potion inside his armour. The potion fizzed out and sloshed all over Louis.

'Ugh! That tickles!' he said.

A moment later Louis had the strangest feeling, like he was growing larger and larger and softer and softer and blobbier and blobbier . . .

BOING

UGH I NEVER WANT TO DO THAT AGAIN.
MARVELLOUS! MARVELLOUS! YOU'RE ON TIME. I DO LIKE IT WHEN PUPILS ARRIVE ON TIME! TIME IS VERY IMPORTANT!
I'M KNIGHT SIR LOUIS.
OH! I KNOW! I KNOW! MARVELLOUS. I'M YOUR HEAD TEACHER, SIR TYMUR TRAFELA. DO COME IN!
I WILL... JUST AS SOON AS I'VE DEFLATED.
HOW WILL YOU DO THAT?
NOT SURE. OH... EXCUSE ME. I'VE GOT A BURP COMING.

CHAPTER 9

Louis had never been to a proper school before. He was excited and frightened all at the same time. What would it be like? Would it be fun? Boring? Would he make friends? Would there be a horrible bully like in all the storybooks he'd read?

The headteacher walked Louis through the school, pointing to things as they went.

'Over there is the Ice-Climbing room. Here's the Sleep-in-a-Blizzard room. That's the Fighting-while-wearing-a-Big-Warm-Coat room. Here's the Survival Kitchen, where you can learn to cook on an ice-cold day.'

Louis scratched his helm, confused. 'Er . . . am

I at the right place? Is this a school for knights? Or for polar explorers?'

'Definitely knights,' confirmed Sir Tymur Trafela. 'Yes, yes.'

'Then why is everything about ice and cold here? I mean, we're on the side of a volcano!'

'Oh, we'll get to that very shortly,' said Tymur as they strode into a large square patch of grass. 'But first I wanted to show you this!'

And Sir Tymur pointed to a MASSIVE statue in the middle of the quad.

Louis stared at it. He couldn't believe what he was seeing. It was a statue of him – Knight Sir Louis – on top of a

huge grey boulder. A large brass metal plate attached to the boulder read: KNIGHT SIR LOUIS! THE GREAT HERO! OUR LAST HOPE!

Suddenly a loud cheer went up and Louis looked around the quad to see lots of other young knights bashing swords against shields and roaring at him.

'Hooray for Louis! Hoorah for our hero! Long live Louis!'

'Er . . .' said Louis to Sir Tymur. 'What's going on?'

CHAPTER 10

Sir Tymur realised he was rushing things. He needed to give Louis time to adjust to his new surroundings. The headteacher lifted his helmet for a moment and smiled. He had a mess of grey curly hair, big bushy eyebrows and a fat moustache. His eyes were deep brown and kind. Well, one of them was. The other one looked like the end of a telescope and was lit up with a blue light.

'Don't panic, Louis,' he said. 'You see, I want you to imagine that the years are passing by like seconds. I want you to imagine we've arrived hundreds of years in the future. There are still knights like you. But they've changed a little. Some have robot arms. Some have robot legs. And some, like me, have robot eyes. I want you to imagine that these knights live in a terrible world where it's always cold and there's a big, nasty baddy ruining everything for everyone. Can you imagine that?'

'Yes. I think so,' said Louis, wondering where this was going.

'And if you were a knight like that, what would you do?'

'I'd find a way to get rid of that big, nasty baddy,' said Louis.

'Exactly!' said Sir Tymur. 'Well, that is exactly our story. We are knights from the future and it's not a very nice place.'

'And you're hoping I can help out?' asked Louis, looking at the statue.

'Exactly,' said Tymur. 'A great cloud of ice and snow is thundering down from the north.

Eventually it will cover the whole world. To begin with, everyone will think it is just a freak storm. But it's really the work of an evil genius – Splint, the Sinister Snowball, Overlord of Brrrrland!'

'I thought Brrrrland was just a made-up place!' said Louis.

'Yes. That's the problem,' agreed Tymur. 'Everyone does. And by the time people work it out, the whole planet will be miles deep in snow. For centuries, heroes have tried to reach Splint and defeat him. But no luck. Even wizards and wizentors are no use as Splint is unaffected by magic.'

'Magic can't defeat him?' asked Louis.

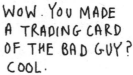
WOW. YOU MADE A TRADING CARD OF THE BAD GUY? COOL.

'Exactly,' said Tymur. He reached into a pocket and handed Louis a trading card (see Chapter Baddy for details!).

'I realised the only way to save the world was to stop this whole thing from ever happening. That meant going back in time!'

'Wow! Bringing a whole school back in time,' said Louis, impressed. 'Must have taken some special magic.'

'It did!' said Tymur and he indicated across the quad. A shiny black cube with flickering, glowing lights slid across the lawn towards him.

'What's that?' said Louis. 'Some sort of future lawnmower?'

'Oh no,' said Sir Tymur, 'that's my friend and wizentor, Dr Kyoob! He's a ninth-generation robot wizard. Sort of like your Clunkalot, but more futurey. Where is Clunkie by the way?'

'He should be following,'

said Louis hopefully as the cube slid up beside them.

'DOOP. BARP. Pleased to meet you. BEEP,' said Dr Kyoob.

'You too,' said Louis, hoping that he was looking at the robot's face and not its bottom.

'I calculated that DARP from all history, you were the BEEP best hero to help us,' said Dr Kyoob.

'That's why we made this statue,' explained Sir Tymur. 'To inspire us.'

'I see,' said Louis. The statue didn't inspire him. It made him worry. He had a lot to live up to!

Dr Kyoob continued, 'I also calculated how to BOOP time-travel our school to your BARP time. But what I cannot calculate is how to DURP defeat Splint. LARP. We need your help, Louis!'

Just then a flap flopped open and a robot hand popped out from the cube holding a sort of sucker.

'Please attach this to your helmet!' said Kyoob.

Louis did as he was asked.

'I will show you the future!' said Kyoob and suddenly Louis felt a thousand pictures rushing in at him.

Here are just a few of them.

'Gosh,' said Louis, shocked. 'The future looks awful!'

'Told you,' said Tymur. 'No one's had a summer holiday in a thousand years!'

'Ugh!' said Louis. 'So, how can I help?'

'Well, I was rather hoping you could tell us,' said Tymur. 'We will train you to survive in the cold, but the rest is up to you.'

'Okay, I'm in,' said Louis. 'I'll work out a plan as we go along.'

'Brilliant!' said Tymur. 'But before you start training, we need to decide which house you're in.'

WHICH HOUSE?
WHAT DOES THAT MEAN?

CHAPTER 11

As far as Louis was concerned, a house was a building that you lived in with your mum and dad. But in school, a house meant something different.

'Every student here belongs to one of four houses,' explained Tymur. 'Sort of like different tribes inside the school that compete against one another. Each one has its own motto, flag, shield, that sort of thing. It's all very traditional!'

He handed Louis an electronic tablet showing the four houses.

Louis scratched his helm and asked, 'Do I just choose which house to join? Or is there some sort of mind-reading hat that chooses?'

'A mind-reading hat? What a funny idea! Oh

no,' said Tymur, 'there's a fun questionnaire. Just fill in the answers.'

Here's one of the questions:

You are stuck in an ice cave with an evil ice wizard. Do you . . .

A. Offer to make the wizard some ginger biscuits, then run away.

B. Challenge the wizard to a duel, then snap his wand in half with one slice of your sword.

C. Spend all day talking about quantum physics until the wizard's brain explodes.

D. Join forces with the wizard and take over the world.

At the end of the quiz, your chosen house is revealed:

REVEAL YOUR HOUSE!

Mostly As – You're a Waffer! Let's make a pot of tea and talk about our favourite sponge pudding.

Mostly Bs – You're a Flapper! Let's slap each other on the back and be pals forever.

Mostly Cs – You're a Beaky! Let's do our sixteen times table and write an essay about it!

Mostly Ds – You're a Squirmin! Let's put itching powder in everyone's underpants.

Louis completed the questionnaire on the electronic pad and pressed FINISH!

A moment later the result appeared on screen. It was just as Louis hoped.

'Looks like you're in Dragonflap!' said Tymur and a huge roar went up from one side of the quad.

'DRAGONFLAP, HO!' shouted everyone in Dragonflap house.

'I knew he was a flapper!' said one of the knights.

'Boo!' shouted someone from the Squirmin side.

Louis looked across at the boo-er. It was a young boy about his own age. His short hair stuck up straight and was cut in such a way that his head looked as though it had a flat top.

'Who's that?' Louis asked the headteacher.

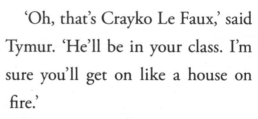

'Oh, that's Crayko Le Faux,' said Tymur. 'He'll be in your class. I'm sure you'll get on like a house on fire.'

Louis wasn't so sure. He had a feeling that if there was a house aflame, it would probably have been set on fire by Crayko.

'Well, come on,' said Tymur. 'It's lesson time! Time to make you into a winter warrior!'

CHAPTER WHOOSH

Let's quickly check in on Clunkalot.

A few hours after Louis had departed for school, Clunkalot's upgrade finished. He looked around to see the lab was empty.

Clunkie spotted Louis' school letter beside the Bopper. He decided to try and follow his master using the same machine. But the Bopper was set for Louis' weight and height, so when Clunkalot launched himself, things didn't go to plan.

SWoooooSH

Clunkalot soared through the air. He soared so fast that he started to heat up. His red paint peeled off revealing the silver metal beneath. He became hotter and glowed yellow. Then hotter still and glowed blue. Then white. Then spotty. Then stripy. Finally, he glowed super red-hot so he sort of looked the same as usual. But you wouldn't want to touch him. Ouch!

He decided to write a poem about this new adventure. It was his best poem ever. He printed it out so he could remember it and show Louis later. But it immediately caught fire and burnt to a crisp.

All this time Clunkie was rising higher above the land. Higher than he'd even been. Higher in fact than anyone or anything had ever travelled before. At last,

SPEEDILY
VELOCITY
METALLICALLY

he popped out of the atmosphere into space and started to cool down. Phew, what a relief!

Clunkie took the time to write another poem.

What's this? This beneath
my heated hooves? A whole world!
But where is my home?

This poem survived, though it did get a little frosty at the edges.

CHAPTER 12

While Clunkalot was heading off on an unexpected space adventure, Pearlin and Catalogue were also having a less than wonderful time. King Burt was still . . .

DOING THINGS DIFFERENTLY.

. . . and making lots of changes around the castle. He had already promoted a giant squirrel to be Captain of the Guard, and made a four-week-old baby Lord of the Royal Bank. He had also decided to rename the days of the week. Unfortunately, he wanted to call them all the same thing.

THE MONTH OF YOGURT

BURTDAY	BURTDAY	BURTDAY	BURTDAY	BURTDAY	BURTDAY	BURTDAY
1	2	3	4	5	6	7
8	9	10	11	12	13	14
15	16	17	18	19	20	21
22	23	24	25	26	27	28

Catalogue and Pearlin guessed he had new ideas in store for them too. They weren't wrong.

'Aha! THERE you are!' said King Burt when he spotted them.

'Uh oh,' they said together.

'I've been looking for you two. Pearlin! I think you've been working as castle wizentor for too long. You need a change.'

'But being a wizentor was my lifelong dream,' said Pearlin wearily.

'Nonsense,' said the king happily, 'I've realised your funny wizard outfit is perfect for something else. From now on, you're going to be the court jester. You can tell us funny stories, sing silly songs and make us all laugh!'

'But I don't want to!' said Pearlin. 'Plus what happens if I need to defend us from some terrible magic spell?'

'Oh, no need to worry about that,' said the king. 'I've appointed a new wizard!'

'What? Who?'

'Catalogue, of course!' said the king, pointing at the stunned boar.

'But I ain't a magical wotsit!' said Catalogue. 'I knows a thing or two or three about weird plants and stuff. That's my bag of tricks. Not magicking or inventing amazing doodars.'

'Decision is made, I'm afraid!' said the king and he strode off, whistling happily to himself.

The next few hours were difficult for Pearlin and Catalogue. Pearlin tried her best to joke around, but her heart wasn't in it.

WHAT DO YOU CALL A WIZARD WITHOUT MAGIC?

I DON'T KNOW, WHAT DO YOU CALL A WIZARD WITHOUT MAGIC?

And Catalogue tried
her trotters at some
magic. But it didn't
go very well.

Then as luck would have it, a letter arrived. It was an invitation for Pearlin.

'This is stone-cold amazing,' she said, impressed. 'I've never been invited before!'

MYSTO THE GRAND WIZENTOR

Invites

PEARLIN

To

THE SPLONG!

The once-a-year very secret conference of Witches, Wizards and Wizentors.

Also welcome . . . Mages, Magicians and Mediums.

Also-also welcome . . . Sorcerers, Sages and Seers.

Also-also-also welcome . . . any people who make animals out of balloons (just amazing, how do you do that?).

Location: well, you know . . . the usual secret place.

Time: well, you know . . . the usual secret time and date.

No plus ones allowed.

Please find enclosed a magic biscuit.
Simply eat and you will be transported to the
secret location.
WARNING!
Eat every crumb or you might
not arrive in the right place!

'What's a plus one?' asked Catalogue.

'That's like a friend, or your animal,' explained Pearlin.

'I see,' said Catalogue. 'So you can't take Mac n Cheese?'

'Sadly, no,' said Pearlin. 'Shame, really, as Mac n Cheese are back from camp today. But I'm not sticking around jestering any more. I'm going to the Splong!'

They both knew the king wouldn't let either of them go anywhere. So, they came up with a cheeky little plan.

CHAPTER

NEWSPAPER

Here is a review of Pearlin and Catalogue's Cheeky
Little Plan in the Castle Newspaper.

Sideways Today
Culture Section
Reviews by Dame Anna Lyzer

Sometimes, you see something so good, you
know you'll remember it forever. This evening,
new court jester Pearlin put on a show like
nothing seen before at Castle Sideways.

She opened with a song and dance number
called Dragon Dance where she pretended to be
a dragon that breathed custard. So very funny,

especially when she covered King Burt from head to toe in Dollop's yellowest custard.

Then she told some very funny jokes about the king.

What do you call a king who only eats baked beans?

King Brrrrrrrrtttttt

What do you call a king with no champion knight?

King Dumb

What do you call a king who makes his wizentor dress up like a jester and do jokes?

A stinky, poopy idiot.

Everyone loved the jokes so much. Except perhaps King Burt.

And then the finale, which none of us shall ever forget! Pearlin brought on an assistant! The new castle wizard, Henrietta Catalogue, now renamed Magic Catalogue (ha ha!) promised she was going to perform a disappearing trick, and she didn't disappoint. Pearlin handed her a piece of parchment and Catalogue read aloud from it.

WIBBLY WOBBLY WOO,
WANGLY GANGLY DOO,
I WILL MAKE US DISAPPEAR,
SO LISTEN ALL YOU WOTSITS HERE
IT'S A BIG GOODBYES
FROM US TO YOU,
ER . . . DINGLY DONGLY DOO!

And then they BOTH VANISHED! And if you missed it, well, sorry but there's no repeat showing because so far . . . both Pearlin and Catalogue have not reappeared! Just amazing! (But also worrying, because now we're without a wizentor. Gulp.)

CHAPTER 13

Pearlin and Catalogue had escaped!

Pearlin had hidden one of her wands up her jester's sleeve. The two of them reappeared outside the castle in their usual outfits and with bags packed for travel. And they were just in time to welcome Mac n Cheese back from their camping trip.

'Right,' said Pearlin, giving her pet dragon a hug. 'I'm off to the Splong. Can you look after Mac n Cheese while I'm gone?'

Catalogue agreed. 'Totally! I think I'll catch a ride to Louis' new school. Maybe they be needing a teacher of weird plants. I could help out and stuff.'

They said their goodbyes and set off on their
separate ways.

Catalogue
was about to head
off on Mac n Cheese when
she smelled something strange in the
air. It smelled like snow! She looked
up and sure enough, hurtling towards
her was a huge snowstorm.

But just a few metres from Castle Sideways,
the storm suddenly disappeared to nothing. The
remaining snow settled out of the sky and fell to
the ground.

'That's a strange old thing,' said Catalogue to
herself. 'For a moment, I thought I saw little faces
in the snow. I must be going doodle-dally.'

And off she flew on Mac n Cheese. But she wasn't going doodle-dally at all.

Five snowballs with faces had fallen out of the storm and rolled close to one another.

CHAPTER 14

Louis took to his winter warrior training like an iced duck to iced water.

His first winter training session was trying to build a house from ice. It was trickier than it sounded. Ice was slippery at the best of times. Trying to cut it into bricks and then get the bricks to stay on top of each other was not easy!

'I say, do you need a hand?' asked a girl with a no-nonsense attitude.

'Yes please,' said Louis. 'I'm Louis, by the way.'

'Oh, I know that,' said the girl, looking at Louis, astonished. 'Seen the statue. Read the book. Got the badge and everything.'

She pointed to a badge on her armour.

Louis gulped. Everyone seemed very sure that he was going to sort everything out. But what if he didn't? He didn't want to disappoint everybody!

'My name's Sir Yuki,' she explained. 'I'm head of Dragonflap House. And this here is my robot owl, 8A-Chip. Call him 8 for short.'

Louis looked across at the owl who shone bright blue, like a polished sapphire.

'Hoot,' said 8. Louis looked at him. The owl didn't hoot like a real owl. He just said *hoot* as though he were a person doing a bad impression of an owl.

'You can stroke him if you like,' said Sir Yuki.

'Pleased to meet you,' said Louis, stroking the owl on the head.

8 said, 'Purr.'

'I didn't know owls purred,' said Louis.

'Sometimes he woofs too,' said Yuki. 'He's funny like that.'

Yuki showed Louis how to cut, lift and position the bricks of ice. Soon they'd made a decent sort of igloo.

'Thanks,' said Louis.

'Anything for a fellow Dragonflapper, and a world-famous hero,' said Yuki, blushing.

'Are you from the future?' asked Louis.

'That's right,' said Yuki, 'and it's really awful. We have to live underground in caves. Some people live in balloon ships flying over the clouds. But that's no better. Everything is just beastly.'

Just then, Crayko Le Faux wandered over. He had a sort of robot bird on his shoulder too. It looked like a large green woodpecker.

'All right, Louis,' said Crayko, 'see you've met boring old Yuki already and her stupid bird.'

'SHUT IT, CRAYKO,' said Yuki. Then she saw Louis' surprised look and said, 'Sorry, Louis. Headteacher says I've got a bit of a temper.'

'I'll say,' said Crayko, sniggering at her.

'Actually, I like 8,' said Louis. 'And Yuki.'

'It's obvious you made a bad choice earlier, joining Dragonflap,' said Crayko. 'Wanted to give you a second chance. Why not come and join us in Squirmin House? We'll teach you how to be a real hero.'

'That's very nice of you,' said Louis, not wanting to get on the wrong side of him. 'But I'm happy in Dragonflap for now.' And because he didn't want to seem ungrateful, he pointed at Crayko's bird and asked, 'Who's this lovely bird, then?'

To his surprise the bird answered itself, 'I'm Peck, you big numpty, and if you don't join Squirmin, I'll chew your nose off.'

'HEY!' said Louis. 'That's not very nice.'

'Clear off, Crayko,' said Yuki. 'You and your nasty cuckoo.'

'I'm not a cuckoo,' said Peck. 'I'm an eagle. Or a hawk. Or something like that.'

'You look like a green woodpecker to me,' said Louis. 'Probably why you're called Peck.'

'No it isn't,' said Peck, before looking confused and saying, 'Is it?'

'Woodpeckers peck holes in trees,' explained Louis.

'What's a tree?' asked Peck. Yuki and Crayko seemed interested too.

'Are you saying there are no trees in the future?' asked Louis.

'Ah! Shut it,' said Peck rudely. 'I know what I am. I'm probably an eagle. I might even be a vampire bat!'

'Bats aren't birds,' said Louis. 'They're more like flying mice or foxes.'

'Are they?' said Peck, sounding less sure of itself again.

'Forget about him,' Crayko said to Peck, turning away. 'Sir Louis is no hero and he's not going to save us. Never was. It's down to us Squirmers.'

Louis watched them walk away. He would have to keep a close eye on Crayko. Then he turned back to Yuki and smiled.

'Right! What's next? I'd love your help with more ice training. If you don't mind?'

'Of course, I don't mind,' said Yuki with a massive grin. 'In fact, I'd mind if you didn't want my help. Come on. Next is skiing lessons. Then skiing while sword fighting. Then skiing while sword fighting in a blizzard. Come on!'

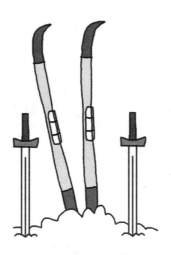

CHAPTER 15

You may remember that when we left Clunkalot in Chapter Whoosh, he was heading into outer space. Well, he's still there.

He is circling the planet and marvelling at what he sees below. It's the perfect adventure for a poet. What a thrill! Right now, he's orbiting closer to the planet's north pole where it is currently night-time. The land below is white with snow and grey with rock. Looking at it makes Clunkie shiver with cold, which is silly because outer-space is even colder.

Clunkalot knows that no one lives this far north. But he knows about the stories of Brrrrrland. And he knows the stories are just stories. It isn't a real place. Right?

Maybe not. He sees a ring of snowy mountains and a land hidden behind them. Why can he see lights twinkling there? Why, when he uses his amazing robot eyes to zoom in, can he see so many little plumes of smoke rising, as though hundreds of people are cooking or keeping themselves warm? Perhaps Brrrrrland is not simply a legend?

Clunkie pops out a poem for himself.

Lands of chills and drifts!
Who is it that calls you home?
Are they warm-hearted?

It's a good question, Clunkie. Who lives there? Are they warm-hearted? Or as cold-hearted as an icicle riding an avalanche?

I'M GOING WITH AVALANCHE.
ME TOO.
NOW, NOW! LET'S NOT JUMP TO CONCLUSIONS.
BRRR. ANYONE FANCY A HOT CHOCOLATE?

CHAPTER 16

Louis was in the middle of a very slippery climbing exercise. He was using an axe and Dave to scale a sheer wall of ice that had been erected on one side of the quad.

'I feel like I'm going to fall,' said Louis, alarmed.

'You can do it!' said Yuki, shouting words of encouragement from the top of the climbing wall.

Crayko was just below him and coming up fast. 'Watch out, Sir Loser,' he said.

IF YOU SO MUCH
AS TOUCH LOUIS,
I'LL KNOCK YOUR
BLOCK OFF!

'Keep your helmet on,' said Crayko with a sneer.

Just then, a dragon with two heads appeared in the sky. Riding on its back was a hairy pig thing.

'WATCH OUT ABOVE,' shouted a student down in the quad.

Yuki looked up in alarm. 'IT'S SOME SORT OF EVIL THINGY!' she shouted, reaching for her sword.

Crayko was stunned too, but he held on. Just because he was a cheat didn't mean he wasn't brave. Peck, on the other hand, was terrified.

'Agh! It's a double headed version of me or something,' said Peck, pressing its claws into Crayko's shoulder.

Crayko shouted in pain, let go and slid right down the icy wall.

SWOOSH WHOOSH

CLONK!

'It's OK,' called Louis with a big smile. 'They're my friends!' It was Catalogue flying in on Mac n Cheese. Their arrival caused quite a sensation as no one from the school had ever seen a real live dragon before, never mind one with two heads. They had never met a boar either, never mind a talking one.

'I'm afraid in the future, dragons are extinct,' explained the headteacher once he realised Catalogue was a friend of Louis'.

'What about piggywigs and boars?' asked Catalogue.

'Don't know,' said Tymur. 'Perhaps they live in the underground mud caves of Splatitton. Not sure. I've never made it there.'

'This far future-or-or-or sounds right rubbish,' concluded Catalogue.

A short while later, Catalogue and Louis were reunited, and they caught up with each other's adventures.

Louis didn't like the sound of the blizzard with faces.

'Nor me,' said Tymur anxiously. 'That means the invasion has begun.'

'But it is not yet BEEP strong enough DARP,' said Dr Kyoob, sliding up to the group.

'Then I need to get going,' said Louis. 'It's time I headed north to face this Splint character.'

'But go where BLARP?' said Dr Kyoob. 'That is our other LEEP problem. We know Splint lives in Brrrrrland somewhere DORP in the north. But we don't FOOP know exactly where. The northlands are KERP vast!'

'Brrrrrland?' said Catalogue. 'I didn't think that place was real!'

'If it's there, I'll find it,' said Louis. 'But I'll need

Clunkalot! Where is he, Catalogue?'

'Eh?' said Catalogue, confused. 'Ain't he here? We thought he'd bopped his way over here days ago.'

'No!' said Louis, suddenly worried. 'I've not seen him. Oh! Where could he be? I might have to go without him.'

'I may be able BOOP to help there DARP,' Dr Kyoob said. 'Come this BEEP way.'

CHAPTER 17

'I've been keeping an DURP eye on the BEEP skies and I spotted this strange BLARP satellite,' said Dr Kyoob. The cube pointed to a horse-shaped dot on one of the screens.

'I think that may be your BOOP horse. In outer space flying around the BEEP planet.'

Louis looked at the dot and said, 'Looks like Clunkie to me. Can I speak to him?'

'Yes, yes FLIRP,' said Kyoob and handed Louis a microphone and pressed a few buttons.

Louis spoke into the microphone uncertainly, 'Clunkalot? Are you there?'

There was a pause and then a piece of paper printed out beside Dr Kyoob. It was a poem.

I was lost, alone
When, at last, winter turned spring
In a friend's return

'Oh, quite beautiful,' said Sir Tymur. 'Gold star from me.'

'It's definitely Clunkie,' said Louis. 'He's the only horse I know that writes haiku poetry.'

Then he spoke into the microphone once more.

'Clunkie. You need to get back down here. We're on Mount Badaboom.'

'I think he's TEEP stuck up there,' said Dr Kyoob.

'He's just forgotten his latest upgrade that's all,' said Louis, then said to his trusty steed, 'Clunkie! ENGAGE STINKY SKUNK MODE!'

Far above the world, in the vastness of space, Clunkalot raised his tail and let out a massive stink. There is no sound in space, so nobody heard it. Lucky, really. Otherwise, it would have been a very noisy and unpleasant sound.

Suddenly, Clunkalot changed course and was heading back to the planet.

Fast.

Very fast.

WATCH OUT, EVERYONE! CLUNKIE'S ABOUT TO CRASH INTO THIS BOOK!

CHAPTER CRASH

WHEEEEEEE
KABOOOOOOM
SCREEEEEECH

Phew! Looks like he put the air brakes on there just in time. Might have blown this book to smithereens. Close one.

CHAPTER 18

You may be wondering what Pearlin has been up to all this time.

I WONDER WHAT PEARLIN HAS BEEN UP TO ALL THIS TIME?

Pearlin had arrived at the meeting of wizards called the Splong. And things were about to go very very wrong.

The Splong is a top-secret meeting of wizentors from across the Many Kingdoms. It only happens once a year. (Unless there is a magical emergency. Then a wizentor can call a What's-Wrong-Come-Along Splong. From time to time, they also have a summer festival called the Ding-Dong-Singalong-A-Song Splong. And there's a sporting event: the Ping-Pong-in-a-Ring Splong. One year they happened at the same time. It was named the What's-Wrong-Come-Along-Ding-Dong-Singalong-A-Song-Ping-Pong-in-a-Ring Splong or WWCADDSASPRS for short.)

This year's Splong had been called by the world's greatest wizentor, Mysto the dwarf. He'd invited the finest wizards.

His old lair had been in Dismal Wood, but that was a very . . . well, dismal, place. His new lair was in Fuming Wood. It sounded like a place to get very angry. But it was really rather lovely (if you didn't mind the stink of sulphur).

I THOUGHT IT WAS INTERESTING.

THANK YOU.

The fumes came from a deep underground river of lava. Hot springs bubbled to the surface making lovely pools of hot water. Mysto had named them the Waters of Illusion and Foresight. Or WIF for short.

All the wizards put on their swimming gear and prepared to get into a big hot pool. But first they collected a glass of Mysto's fresh lemonade. He'd even laid on a huge bucket of ice cubes to cool their drinks.

'You're spoiling us, Mysto,' said one wizard.

'The best Splong ever!' said another.

It was all new to Pearlin but she was having a great time. Pearlin grabbed a lemonade for herself and took the ice tongs (Splong tongs) to pick up an ice cube. She selected the biggest one she could find and plopped it into her glass. It wasn't really cube shaped. It was round and more like a ball of snow. In fact, it didn't fit in the glass, but sat on top of it.

'Oh well,' Pearlin thought. 'It'll melt in a minute.'

She too climbed into the hot, relaxing waters.

Mysto bashed a gong.

PROBABLY CALLED THE SPLONG GONG.

YOU'RE NOT WRONG.

GOOONNNGG!

'Thank you all for coming along to the Splong,' said Mysto. 'And welcome to brand-new member, Pearlin.'

'Wotcha,' said Pearlin, raising her glass to everyone.

'This year's Splong was due to happen next month, but I thought we should get together now.'

'Yes, I did notice that,' said a grumpy, old wizard called Gordon Fossil-Beard. 'I had to cancel my holiday. Not happy.'

'Well I'm sorry, Gordon, but this is important,' said Mysto. 'Has anyone else noticed strange things happening with snow and ice?'

'Yes, yes, yes,' agreed Hagatha Squint. 'Just the other day, I left my house for a bit of shopping, but when I came home it was buried under a hill of snow. I thought I must have left a spell running.'

'And just yesterday,' said another wizard called Tiny Michael, 'I was riding home on Mayo, my mouse. We were suddenly picked up by a freezing whirlwind. I leapt to safety, but poor Mayo's gone.

Carried away.' Tiny Michael rubbed a tear from his eye.

'Actually, now you mention it,' said Gordon Fossil-Beard, 'it started snowing indoors this week. I thought that was a bit odd.'

'We need to find out who's behind all this,' said Mysto, 'and stop them before it's too late.'

'It's already too late,' said a voice.

Everyone looked at Pearlin.

'Don't look at me,' she said, confused. 'I didn't say nothing.'

'She's right,' said the snowball on top of her glass. It rolled around to reveal a nasty, little face.

CHAPTER 19

It was Flint, one of the Sinister Snowball's little siblings! He smiled, showing off a set of very pointy, icicle teeth. As he spoke, the air around him frosted and crackled.

'I'll say it again. It's already too late! Unless . . . one of you would like to come and work for my big brother, Splint, Overlord of Brrrrland, the Sinister Snowball himself!'

'Not on your nelly,' said Mysto, and he raised his hand to cast a spell. But of course, he wasn't holding his wand. He was holding a glass of lemonade, which, although delicious, was not at all magical.

'Ha ha! Thought as much,' said Flint, before screaming, 'LET'S DO IT, SNOWBALLS!'

Suddenly four other snowballs leapt from the ice bucket. Mint, Hint, Clint and Sharon were on the rampage.

Before the wizards could jump out and find a wand, the five snowballs each spat out tiny shards of ice which shot up the wizards' noses, down their throats and headed straight for their hearts.

IS THAT THE ONE WHERE A LITTLE BOY SWALLOWS A WHOLE MIRROR AND THEN GOES OFF TO LIVE WITH A GIANT ICE CREAM UNTIL HIS SISTER TURNS UP AND RUNS A WARM BATH?

SORT OF.

Unfortunately, the snowballs had never actually tried out the ice shard thing before. The shards were SO cold that they didn't just freeze the wizards' hearts. They froze the wizards' bodies too. And the pool they were sitting in.

Mint looked at Clint. 'Oops. We're in for it now,' he said. 'The boss isn't going to be happy.'

'Can we heat them up and have another go?' suggested Hint, staring at all the frozen wizards.

'No good,' said Flint. 'They'll be ready for us.'

'Hang on,' said Sharon. 'This one's not frozen.'

They turned to look at Pearlin. It was true.

Pearlin blinked, opened her ice-blue eyes and looked at the snowballs.

'So, wizard. Are you one of us?' asked Flint.

'I am. I serve the one true master, the Sinister Snowball,' said Pearlin harshly.

'Good,' said Flint. 'At least we have one wizard to do magic! Now it's time to return home!'

The snowballs gathered around Pearlin and began to roll around her in a circle. Faster and faster until there was a freezing whirlwind. Then SHOOOOOF, they were gone, flying away in an icy twister. Only a pile of snow remained. And a whole bunch of frozen wizards, of course.

CHAPTER ONESIE

So, you may be wondering why Pearlin didn't freeze completely like the other wizards. Well, it's all thanks to her dragon-skin swimming onesie.

SCIENCEY BIT

Pearlin lives with dragon Mac n Cheese.

Did you know that when dragons grow, they do so in stages?

Just like snakes, when they get too big for their skin, they shed it!

Then they expand, and their new skin dries.

The dragon skin that is left behind can be used to make clothes.

Like this amazing vest, tights, or swimming onesie!

Pearlin's dragon onesie had partly protected her from the ice attack! Sadly, it hadn't stopped the ice from piercing her heart and turning it cold and nasty.

And so, for the first time ever, the fate of the world had been thrown into terrible danger . . . by a onesie.

CHAPTER 20

A couple of days later, everything was ready for Louis' polar adventure. It was all reported in the school newsletter.

A message from Sir Tymur Trafela, headmaster

It is with great pleasure that we announce the graduation of pupils, Sir Louis and Sir Yuki. They will be going off on an adventure to save the world. We wish them all the very best and hope to see them at this year's summer ball (assuming there is another summer ever again).

Knight Sir Louis

Brave knight with cold weather gear.

Dave the Sword

Magic sword. Happy to have a new hat.

Catalogue

Plucky friend, ready to go anywhere. Expert in plants.

Clunkalot

Repainted blue to blend in with wintry conditions.

Knight Sir Yuki

Head of Dragonflap House. Never been on a real adventure. Ready for anything. Bit shouty sometimes.

We also wish 8 the owl well on his mission. He'll be heading south and telling anyone he meets to prepare for an eternal winter. Just in case everything goes wrong.

Knight Sir Louis and his friends stepped outside the school, ready for their mission to find and stop the Sinister Snowball.

'Here's the plan,' Louis said to the headmaster. 'We go ahead as a small scouting party. We should be able to sneak into Brrrrrland like spies and find out what's going on. Once we know what's what, we'll send word and all the Knights of the Future School can follow.'

'Sounds good to BEEP me,' said Dr Kyoob.

'Agreed,' said Sir Tymur. 'We'll keep training. We'll be ready!'

'The first challenge we face is to find Brrrrrland,' said Louis. 'We haven't the faintest idea where it is!'

126

'Oh spuds,' said Catalogue. 'This is going to be the longest adventure since Sir Slow went on a trip to Slowland in his Slowmobile.'

But Catalogue didn't need to worry. One of his companions knew exactly where to find Brrrrrland. Clunkalot. Because he'd seen it from outer space! He printed out a lovely aerial map for them to follow.

'Wow!' said Louis. 'This is really going to save some time. Amazing work, Clunkie! Let's go!'

CHAPTER 21

If there was a holiday advertisement for Brrrrrland it might look something like this . . .

WELCOME TO BRRRRRLAND!
SO MANY PLACES TO SEE

Why not Climb Mount Razor? Be the first person to survive the journey! Do you like sharp rocks? Strong winds? If you make it, draw some pictures and bring them back. We'd love to know what it's like.

Take a Snow Trek through the Snow Cheese Valley. Wondering why it's named after cheese? No, not because it stinks! Ha ha! It's because of the massive holes everywhere. A thrilling trip of a lifetime. Must be a great place to visit because everyone that went down a hole has NEVER returned.

Visit the Frozen Forest of Giant Nasty Gnats. Remember to take your insect spray. And some armour. And maybe a flamethrower. Some guests even get to take a ride on one of the gnats! Must be thrilling. Or terrifying. You decide!

Take a Mammoth Ride through the Massive Icicle Valley. Enjoy the comfort of riding on a huge, stinky, hairy elephant thing. They'll take you on a trek through the massive icicle valley.

Don't make any loud noises though or it might start raining giant sticks of pointy ice! Ha ha ha ha ha ha ha ha. Hmm. No, seriously. Be quiet.

If you want to actually survive your visit to Brrrrland, you can simply stay in our capital city. That's what we all do. Of course, you'll have to follow the rules. There are a lot of rules. Our very nice Overlord, Leader and President Splint makes new laws and rules every few days. Just make sure you do as you're told. At. All. Times.

P.S. Splint is such a great leader. Really nice. Just lovely. He's ace. The best. We love him. Honest.

CHAPTER 22

Louis and Yuki raced through the air on Clunkie while Catalogue flew beside them on Mac n Cheese. Mount Badaboom and the school faded into the distance behind them.

Until now, Yuki had never left the school grounds. Her mouth hung open in amazement as she looked down. In the far future where she was from, the world was covered in miles of snow. But here, in this time, there were fluffy green forests, colourful swaying farm fields, rivers like blue ribbons and pretty country houses with thatched roofs.

'I never dreamed the world could be so beautiful,' she said.

'It's right nice, ain't it?' agreed Catalogue. 'Shame to see it turn into a ball of ice.' She patted a cloth bag of something over her shoulder. 'I'm hoping these lovely wotsits will help us on our big old quest.'

'What are you carrying, Catalogue?' asked Louis.

Catalogue reached inside her bag and pulled out a sample of the plants she'd picked from the slopes of Mount Badaboom.

CHILLIES MAGMA ROOTS GLOWIN MUSHROOMS LAVA WORMS FLAMIN FLOWERS

'Fascinating,' said Yuki. 'What will you use them for?'

'Dunno yet,' said Catalogue. 'But I'm doing a guess that having hot stuff like this will be right useful somewhere soon.'

'Good thinking, as usual,' said Louis with a smile.

After a while, Louis and his band of friends could see the snow line. It stopped just north of Castle Sideways.

'Should we stop here for the night?' asked Yuki, keen to see Louis' home.

'I'm thinking that's a chunky no,' suggested Catalogue. 'King Burt's got some funny ideas going on at the moment.'

'That's true,' said Louis looking down at his home far below. 'But we can do a fly-by, just to give Yuki a better look.'

They flew in low and circled around Castle Sideways.

But King Burt happened to be looking out of his window in the Great Hall. For some reason, he had longer hair than usual. His moustache was looking much untidier too. He spotted Louis and the flying band and immediately shouted out some orders.

'I say, Sir Louis, I order you to come home and become Lord of Moustaches. I need a new barber! Mine has run off!'

In fact, almost everyone had run off. The courtiers hadn't liked the king's new ideas very much and had all 'gone on holiday'.

'And you, Catalogue,' shouted King Burt. 'I'm going to make you Lady in Charge of Dusting the Royal Throne! THAT'S AN ORDER!'

Louis and Catalogue looked at one another. They knew it was important to obey the king. But neither of them wanted to oversee moustaches or dust. Especially when the world needed saving.

'Can you hear what the king is saying?' said Louis to Catalogue, winking.

'Wot? Me? Can't hear nothing nowhere!' said Catalogue, getting the hint.

'Let's go, before we do hear,' said Louis and once more Clunkie and Mac n Cheese rose high in the air and headed north.

They crossed over the snowline. The air instantly became chilly.

'Here we come, Brrrrrland,' shouted Louis.

Far below in Castle Sideways, King Burt huffed and puffed, annoyed.

'What's the matter with everyone?' he said out loud. 'Where has everyone gone?'

'Excuse me, Mr King,' said an unfamiliar voice, 'are you looking for your people?'

Burt turned to look for the speaker. There was no one there. But someone had thrown a snowball onto the floor in front of him. He picked it up ready to throw it out of the window. To his surprise, it had a face and it spoke to him.

'Hello, Mr King. My name is Mint. Would

you like to see where your courtiers have gone?'

'Oh, yes please,' said the king.

A short moment later King Burt was carried up
in a whirlwind of snow and ice.

CHAPTER 23

aka

CHAPTER SUSPICION.

In this chapter, we're feeling suspicious. That means we have the feeling that someone is up to something naughty.

We are suspicious that someone is following our heroes Louis, Yuki and Catalogue.

Here are some likely suspects.

Please tick all boxes that you think apply.

☐ Crayko Le Faux

☐ Peck

☐ Sharon the snowball

☐ Whiffling Doob the Wonder Horse

CHAPTER 24

Louis marvelled at the strangeness of the world below. Places he knew well were covered in a thick blanket of snow. Far off to the east he could see the desolate land of Dooooooom! Usually it smoked from all the dragons setting it alight. But now it steamed as the snow settled on the hot land. And the town of Soggy Hoo, which usually had a rain cloud over it, now had a large snow cloud.

They flew on over the land of Klaptrap and over the Principality of Plopp. Further and further north they flew, until far ahead they saw a great ring of mountains like an enormous shark's jaw. Clunkie printed out a poem.

A mouth of mountains
Marks the border of Brrrrrland
Winter waits beyond

'Now's the perfect time to sneak over the border,' said Louis to the others. 'The sky is clear. We can fly right up and over the ring of mountains.'

But as they raced on, clouds started to form over Brrrrland. The closer they came, the worse the weather became. The wind whipped up to a frantic storm. The air chilled below freezing.

'It's no good,' said Louis, anxiously. 'We won't make it.'

'Too right,' agreed Catalogue. 'We'll be frozen into people popsicles if we keep this up. You'll have to start calling me the Winter Catalogue.'

'Let's find somewhere to camp,' said Louis. 'Any suggestions, Yuki? How do you camp in a snow storm?'

'Let's see if we can find a cave,' she said, and they dropped down and skirted over the mountainside.

It was no good, they couldn't see much in the whiteout of the wind and snow.

'Hey there,' shouted Catalogue at Louis. 'I got a

fresh idea. Why not get us some walruses to find a spot? They like cold and that, don't they?'

'Great idea!' said Louis.

Not everyone has the power to summon walruses. But Dave does. When the wind whips across his blade, he sings. And when he sings, walruses come to listen. And they arrive very quickly.

Louis unsheathed his sword and held Dave up into the storm wind.

Dave sliced the air. He sang, very off-key. It sounded awful. It made the others feel very strange. Louis and Yuki felt sick. Catalogue felt her ears trying to jump off her head. Mac n Cheese thought they might explode. Clunkic felt his batteries draining.

But the walruses came. They appeared on the mountainside (via walrus wormholes – see *Knight Sir Louis and the Dreadful Damsel* for details!)

They liked the sound of Dave. They liked it a lot.

Louis flew down on Clunkie and called out to the walruses.

'Would you like to meet Dave in person? If you find us a cave, I can arrange it!'

The walruses were starstruck. Meet Dave? Their musical hero! Wow! They got to work and flipped and flopped and flubbed all over the mountain until they found a cave for the heroes. It had a small entrance but was long and deep so the wind and snow couldn't get too far inside.

As soon as they were inside, the wind stopped

flying over Dave's blade and he stopped singing. Louis and his friends were relieved.

And for once, the walruses didn't mind either. They formed a long queue and, one by one, they all had the chance to meet Dave. After an hour or so, they flopped away again feeling very, very happy.

CHAPTER CAVE

The heroes settled down for the night.

'This is nice,' said Catalogue, 'if your idea of nice be living inside a dark, spooky rock.'

'It's pretty cold too,' said Louis. 'Mac n Cheese, can you help?'

Mac n Cheese rolled a few loose rocks into a pile and breathed fire onto them. They soon glowed red hot.

'How simply wonderful!' said Yuki. 'Wish we had dragons in the future.'

Then Louis took some survival supplies and made them dinner. Meanwhile, Clunkie lingered at the cave mouth.

'You okay, Clunkie?' asked Yuki.

'Probably doing a poem,' suggested Catalogue.

But for once, Clunkalot wasn't thinking about poetry. He was looking out into the night and wondering about some strange movements in the storm. He zoomed in with his robot eyes and took some photos.

'Looks like we're being followed,' said Yuki through gritted teeth.

'What's his plan?' wondered Catalogue. 'He hoping to join our team here?'

Louis said, 'I doubt it. He's no fan of Dragonflap.'

Crayko was struggling against the surprise storm.

Louis sighed. He couldn't leave him out there, even if he was up to mischief. 'I think we should help him.'

This was too much for Yuki who suddenly

exploded. 'CRAYKO'S SUCH A SQUIRMING SLIMEBALL.'

The cave rumbled and echoed with her voice. The disturbance made the snow around the cave fall in a huge FLUMP, blocking the cave mouth.

'Uh-oh,' said Catalogue.

'Aw! Sorry,' said Yuki.

'On the plus side,' said Louis, looking at the solid wall of snow, 'it's not as windy.'

CHAPTER 25

And now, we interrupt this book for a message from Supreme Overlord Splint.

Hello, reader. I am very pleased to meet you. I wish to assure you that I am not some kind of bad guy. I am no villain. This book is full of lies about me. I am in fact a very fair, lovely and smiley leader of the great country of Brrrrrland. Isn't that right, Prime Minister Crunch?

HUH? WHAT DID YOU SAY, BOSS?

I can prove that I am fair. Every five years we have elections to see who will be the next leader. In the last election it was a choice between me or a chocolate bar called Kevin. Sadly, at the last moment, Kevin was eaten. Some say he was eaten by my bodyguard, Iggy the ice golem. Some say I told Iggy to eat Kevin. This is not true. There is no evidence. Apart from the video recording.

152

But that is a fake video. How do I know? Because I am an expert in making fake videos.

Just believe me. I order you to believe me. Er . . .

Anyway, the people voted for me and I became the leader once again. Thank you to the people of Brrrrrland for trusting me once more.

I want to tell you how lovely Brrrrrland is. It is the best place in the whole world. How do I know? Because when I was a little snowball I travelled the world. Everywhere I went, people said mean things about the winter. Things like . . .

Ugh! It's so horrible and cold.

I can't wait for winter to end.

Winter is so boring.

Those people don't know what they are talking about. Winter is the best! And because I know it is, I want to bring winter to the whole world! I want to cover the whole planet in a pillow of white snow! Forever. Yes, Brrrrrland will be everywhere. And I will be its lovely and smiley leader!

Don't just take my word for it ... here are some other people who agree with me.

That is the end of this public message.

CHAPTER 26

Louis and his friends were stuck in the cave and wondering how to get out.

'At least we're hidden,' said Louis. 'No one knows we're here.'

But that wasn't exactly true. The mountain wasn't quite as solid as it appeared. The mountain was in fact a network of tunnels and caves occupied by goblins.

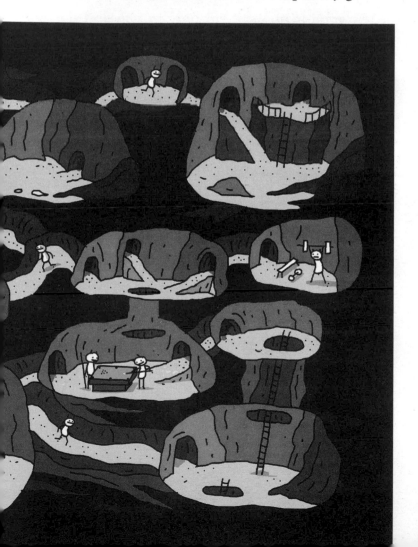

People don't like goblins. People tell nasty stories about them. People know that goblins creep about in the dark. People say that goblins are ugly.

The funny thing about these 'people' is that they haven't actually met any goblins.

Yes, goblins might seem ugly to you and me. Even scary! But they find each other quite beautiful. And even though they enjoy living in tunnels under mountains, they are some of the friendliest and most helpful folk.

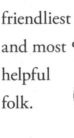

The goblins of Mount Sawtooth could tell someone had arrived in one of their caves.

'Okay, everyone, group meeting,' said a chunky

goblin called Zob. 'We have unexpected guests and they may need rescuing.'

'Maybe we should leave them be,' said another goblin called Yob. 'Last time we did a cave rescue, it was for those dwarves. They thought we were attacking them. It was a disaster. I barely got away with my head!'

Some of the other goblins nodded and agreed: 'Yeah, yeah. True. I remember.'

'Okay, good point, Yob,' said Zob. 'So, let's make sure they know we're friendly. Any suggestions? How can we do that?'

The other goblins pondered the question. Mob put her hand up.

'We could smile a lot?' she suggested.

'Good, good,' said Zob.

Another goblin, Shob said 'Why don't we sing them a nice song?'

'Oo! I like that,' said Zob.

'We could take them some presents,' said Vob.

'Brilliant,' said Zob. 'Let's do all of those!'

The only problem with this plan was this . . .

WHEN GOBLINS SMILE THEY SHOW OFF THEIR POINTY TEETH →

CLANGETY CLANG

← GOBLIN SONGS ARE VERY SHOUTY AND THEIR INSTRUMENTS VERY CLANGY.

A GOBLIN'S IDEA OF A GOOD PRESENT IS A POINTY ROCK. →

A short while later, Louis was resting with his friends Catalogue, Clunkie and Yuki. Louis had his head on the tail of dragon Mac n Cheese. It made for a very warm pillow. In his dreamy state he thought he saw the back of the cave open up. An instant later a hoard of goblins ran in shouting, flashing their teeth, and waving rocks around.

AGGGHHH!

CHAPTER 27

Louis, Catalogue, Clunkie and Yuki were sure
the goblins were attacking.
They jumped up ready to fight.
Everything might have gone
very badly for Louis' band of
friends and the goblins if it hadn't
been for Mac n Cheese. The double-
headed dragon woke up and unfurled,
ready to defend Louis and the others.

In an instant the goblins had all thrown
themselves onto the dragon. But they weren't
attacking Mac n Cheese. They were cooing and
cuddling and stroking. Luckily, the word for
dragon is pretty much the same in all languages.

DROOG'GEEN

This unexpected turn of events gave Catalogue some of what she called 'brain thinky time'. And she was very good at languages.

'Hangs on a fair moments,' said Catalogue. 'That roaring what these goblins was doing just now. I thinks it was some manner of sing-song. If I'm not mistaken it went something like this . . .'

'Or something like that,' said Catalogue.

Her singing had caught the attention of Yob.

'You can understand us?' said Yob.

'Sort of. Ish,' agreed Catalogue.

'Do you need our help to get out of this cave? We can dig you a hole through the snow,' said Mob.

'That's very nicely of you,' said Catalogue. 'But we is actually trying to get into Brrrrrland. Trouble is, it's not as easy as snuffling out a mushroom.'

'Oh!' said Vob. 'Well, if you're mad enough to want to go to Brrrrrland, we can show you a much easier way.'

A short while later, Louis, Catalogue, Yuki,

Clunkie and Mac n Cheese were happily walking through the goblin tunnels.

It turned out that the goblins didn't like living in the dark. They loved things to be lit up. But Splint's long winter had chilled right through to the heart of the mountain and their candles just wouldn't stay lit. Dragon fire doesn't go out easily so the goblins had been very happy to see the two-headed dragon. Slowly but surely, Mac n Cheese helped to light up the goblins' underground community.

The goblins hadn't always spent all their days and nights under the mountain. In the old days, they'd roamed all over Brrrrland. But Splint had made life so unpleasant they'd decided just to stay indoors.

After a couple of hours, the heroes had been led through the mountain to the other side. Here a small cave mouth led out into Brrrrrland.

'Thank you, goblins,' said Louis in their language. He'd managed to pick up some basics from Catalogue.

'I wonder,' said Zob, 'could Mac n Cheese stay with us for a bit? Help light up the rest of the place?'

Catalogue translated and Louis agreed.

'Okay. Mac n Cheese can wait here. Might be tricky to hide a dragon where we're going,' he admitted.

'Don't worry, me lovelies,' said Catalogue, stroking Mac n Cheese's back. 'We're not going to forgets you.'

'That's right,' said Louis to the double-headed dragon. 'And if we get in big trouble, maybe you'll be able to swoop in and save us!'

Louis and his band of adventurers headed into Brrrrland.

Mac n Cheese waved them goodbye and sighed sadly. Little wisps of smoke escaped their noses.

The goblins waved the heroes goodbye too.

'Good luck,' said Zob.

'Have a lovely time,' said Gob.

'Do you think they'll survive?' wondered Shob.

'Not a chance,' said Zob.

CHAPTER 28

Knight Sir Louis smiled to himself as he walked down a steep gorge in the mountainside with Yuki, Catalogue and Clunkie. This was the life. Adventure! They had made it into the frozen land of Brrrrrland. And like all his favourite past missions, he had his friends by his side.

TOLD YOU!

SO BRRRRRLAND DOES EXIST AFTER ALL.

ALRIGHT. DON'T GO ON ABOUT IT.

All Louis had to do now was find Splint the Sinister Snowball and stop him from turning the world into an ice planet. That may sound easy to you.

NO, NOT REALLY.

Well, you're right. It wasn't going to be easy at all. But Louis liked a challenge.

He was thinking out loud. 'So, we know Splint wants to freeze the planet. We know WHY. He wants to rule over everything forever. But we don't know HOW he's creating these super-blizzards. I wonder if it's some sort of magic?'

Louis felt in his pocket and pulled out the Splint trading card. He remembered that Splint had no magic, and couldn't be defeated by magic.

'If it is magic,' he said, 'it'll be someone else doing it for him.'

'If only we had Pearlin,' said Catalogue. 'Maybe she'd be knowing who it was.'

'First things first, we need to find Splint,' said Louis. 'We need to spy on him for a bit. I wonder where he lives?'

'Could be anywheres,' said Catalogue, 'top of a mountain, under the snows, in a massive ice palace.'

'NO. COR. WOWSERS!' said Yuki loudly, before suggesting, 'I bet Splint has some sort of enormous ski lodge.'

'An enormous ski lodge? What's making you think that?' asked Catalogue.

They had reached the end of the gorge. Below them was the capital city of Brrrrrland.

Catalogue was fascinated by the flower. It was like a huge daisy with white petals and a dark centre. She wanted to get a closer look. Perhaps it was a new species? She might be able to name it after herself and her friends. She was thinking of calling it *Bigus adventurii*.

'We can't just walk into the city,' said Louis. 'We need to blend in. What can you see down there, Clunkie?'

Clunkie used his telescopic eyes to get a close look at the inhabitants of the city. Louis opened up Clunkie's side hatch, sat inside and turned on the little display screen. It showed all that Clunkie could see.

'Hey, what's that shop over there? Look!' said Louis.

Clunkie zoomed in:

'Yes!' said Louis. 'Once we work out how to get down there, it's time to go shopping!'

'YES! LET'S DO SHOPPING!' said Yuki at the top of her voice.

It dislodged a pile of snow above them which rushed down the gorge towards them.

'Uh oh,' she said, 'sorry about that.'

Louis shouted, 'Everyone inside Clunkie, NOW!'

Catalogue, Yuki and Louis crushed themselves inside Clunkie's belly.

A moment later the snow biffed into Clunkalot and sent him sliding at top speed down the mountain. It was a new experience. Clunkalot felt moved to write a haiku.

The wild world whooshes
The avalanche, it rushes
We crash through bushes

CHAPTER 29

Louis and his friends were stuck in a pile of snow at the edge of the city. By the time they had dug themselves out it was night-time. They tiptoed through the quiet streets, hiding from any passers-by. Soon, they reached the Fancy Dress shop which was closed for the day. Louis clonked the bells outside, but not too loudly. Nothing happened. He tried again a little louder. A light came on inside and then the door opened. A small yeti answered the door. She eyed them with four intelligent wily eyes.

'How can I help you, good sir?' said the yeti. 'And may I say how lovely your suit of armour is. Very shiny.'

Ludmila the yeti could tell a good customer a mile off. It paid to be polite.

'Sorry to disturb you when you're closed,' said Louis. 'But we'd like to buy some costumes.'

'We're er ... tourists,' said Yuki, fibbing a bit, 'but we don't want to stand out. We want to blend in.'

'That's right-o,' said Catalogue. 'We is just passing through like a log floating down a river of life. We're not here to find Splint and stop the end of the world. No ways.'

'I see,' said Ludmila. 'Don't worry. I'm sure we can find just what you need. Come in.'

'So, is it fun times for your business?' asked Catalogue, trying to seem like a normal customer.

'Not really,' said Ludmila. 'Our supreme overlord Splint has been rounding up more and more people to help in the ice mine. Including my customers. Almost got me too, but I pretended to be one of my own costumes.'

'Clever,' said Louis, who sensed that Ludmila might not be very happy with her supreme overlord.

They walked into her showroom. It was impressive.

They tried out a few options . . .

Louis paid Ludmila some gold coins for her trouble. Her four eyes almost popped out on stalks.

'Cor, real gold!' said Ludmila. 'Round these parts, the money's usually rocks and ice. Nice to have some real money for once.'

Finally, they headed back out of the shop and Ludmila turned off the lights. She waved them goodbye from the doorstep.

'I hope you won't tell anyone about us,' said Louis. 'You know, because we're tourists and we just want to blend in.'

'Of course not,' said Ludmila kindly. 'I wouldn't dare tell anyone that two knights, a talking boar and a robot horse are sneaking about. Wink wink. Good luck with your mission. And by the way, the quickest route to the Great Lodge is down Frostbite Lane.'

CHAPTER 30

Early next morning, Splint the Sinister Snowball, Supreme Overlord of Brrrrland, rolled into the Great Lodge's meeting hall and into his huge leather chair. He liked his chair. It made him feel even more important than usual. Also present were Prime Minister Crunch the carrot, Iggy the ice golem and the guards. The five snowballs were there too.

'I have a joke for everyone,' Splint said loudly.

Prime Minister Crunch started laughing.

HA HA
HA HA
HA HA
HA HA

'Shut up, you idiot!' Splint ordered. 'I haven't told it yet.'

Prime Minister Crunch stopped laughing.

'What do you call a dance party in a blizzard?'

'WE DON'T KNOW, SUPREME OVERLORD,' said everyone together.

Sharon knew the answer.

Fortunately, Splint didn't hear her. He loudly announced the punchline to the waiting room with glee. 'A snowball.'

TOLD YOU!

Everyone started laughing again. This time Splint smiled and nodded. After about five minutes of everyone laughing non-stop, he suddenly said, 'OKAY! QUIET!'

Everyone obeyed immediately.

'So, what's on my agenda today?' asked Splint.

Prime Minister Crunch stepped forward and said, 'The new wizard, your supreme-ness.'

'Oh yes,' recalled Splint. He was due to meet his new wizard, the frozen-hearted Pearlin. He was hoping she could solve his problem.

Pearlin was brought in by a guard, her ice-blue eyes gleaming.

'New wizard, I really want to take over the whole world,' explained Splint. 'I think I'd be really good at it.'

'So, what's holding you back?' asked Pearlin frostily.

'Our blizzards just didn't reach far enough,' said Splint. 'We've had this blizzard-making machine for decades. Made by some crazy weather-wizard in the ice mine. I ordered the machine to be turned to maximum but it was too old. It just puttered out to nothing and fell to pieces.'

'Right!' said Pearlin. 'So, what you need is a NEW mind-blowing invention. A new mega, super, giant blizzard-making machine. Something like . . . hmm . . . this.'

She sketched out her idea on a block of ice using a chisel.

'I think I'll call it the Blizzo Blaster,' said Pearlin, her eyes gleaming blue. 'But I'll need a large, open space to build it. And a load of people to help get it done.'

'Ooo, yes, yes, yes. This is it!' said Splint greedily. 'Get started straight away. Build it in the ice mine beneath the Great Lodge. There are plenty of new prisoners who will want to help, if they know what's good for them.'

Pearlin didn't waste any time. She headed straight out of the lodge and marched towards the ice mine.

CHAPTER 31

Outside, close by the lodge, were two yetis, one penguin and a woolly rhino.

Yes, you've guessed it. It was Louis and his chums.

Louis and Yuki were trying to find a sneaky way into the lodge.

Catalogue was mostly interested in the big white flower.

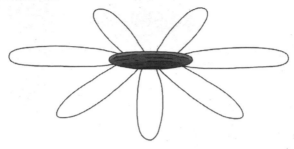

'Don't look like a real flower,' said Catalogue, disappointed. It had no stalk. The petals simply lay on the ground. 'There goes my idea of giving it a nice name. And what's more, I think the middle is not part of the flower but a whopping great big hole. Wonder where that goes?'

Before Louis could reply, he saw Pearlin come out of the lodge.

'Hey, it's Pearlin,' said Catalogue. She waved and shouted, 'COO-EE!'

Louis was excited too. 'Heya! Pearlin! It's us . . . it's . . .'

Louis trailed off. Something wasn't right.

'Wait!' he said. 'What's Pearlin doing here?'

But it was too late. Pearlin had heard Catalogue and came over. She looked at the yetis, the penguin and the rhino.

'What did you say?' said Pearlin coldly. 'How do you lot know my name?'

Louis saw that her eyes had changed colour to ice blue and her hair had frost around the edges. She wasn't wearing her usual smile either.

'Err . . . oh, we was told by an icy thingy,' said Louis, quickly disguising his voice.

'A snowball? Which one? I bet it was that Sharon! It wasn't that stupid carrot Crunch, was it?'

'Yeah,' said Louis. 'That Sharon. Or Crunch. Or someone.' Louis hadn't the faintest idea who Sharon or Crunch were. He just hoped Pearlin would believe in their disguises.

'I wonder if we could meet the big boss?' Louis asked, pushing his luck. 'Would he come out and see us? It would make our century!'

'Never in a million years,' barked Pearlin, her eyes flashing. 'Everyone knows Splint the Supreme Overlord never leaves his lodge. There might be enemies lying in wait. And who knows what they'll look like. Maybe they'll look like you lot!'

Pearlin eyed them suspiciously. There was something about them that seemed familiar. Especially that woolly rhino. She had the strangest feeling that she had designed and built it. (Her instincts were right. Clunkalot was one of her inventions!)

Pearlin shook her head and dismissed the feeling.

'In fact, why don't you come along with me?' she said silkily. 'I have a job for you.'

And before Louis and the others could complain, they were surrounded by ice golems and being marched towards the ice mine.

CHAPTER 32

Elsewhere, Crayko Le Faux had been keeping a diary. Not a written diary. It's one of the advantages of having a robot woodpecker. You can ask it to record what you're saying.

Okay, Peck. You recording?
Recording.
So. It's Thoosday the . . . something. It's hard to keep up with all this time travel.
Yeah. Who cares what day it is?
Anyway. Louis and Yuki and their piggywig get to go off on an adventure!
What about me? Not fair! Pooh!
Yeah. Pooh.

That's why we're going to sneak after them, find this Splint and win the day for Squirmin House.

Yeah. That'll show 'em. I'm staying here, right?

Of course not, Peck. You're coming too.

But it sounds really dangerous.

Of course. You're not afraid, are you?

Me?

Think of all the robot crackers you'll get from everyone when you're a hero.

Oo, yes. Okay. I'm not afraid any more.

You're sure about that? I don't want some scaredy bird with me!

Who's afraid? Not me. But I'm only going if you are.

Good.

So, how are we getting there?

Let's take the Flying Motorbike.

Nice.

End recording.

Recording.

Yep. Cor. It's cold up here.

Louis has no idea we're after him. We're so clever.

Yeah. Clever. And cold.

And we're near some big mountains and there's some sort of storm coming.

Let's shelter in a cave.

No! Let's ride through it! It'll be a blast!

I think my idea's better.
Here goes! End recording.

Recording. Are you recording, Peck?
Huh? Oh. Yeah. Where are we?
I think we're in a bag.
A bag?
Last thing I remember is the storm. We
rode into it. Bike was whirled around.
Think we must have crash landed on the
mountain. What a blast! Go Squirmin
House!
So, whose bag are we in?
Use that beak of
yours to make a
hole, will you?
Nnn. Grr.
Nnn. Cor.
It's tough
stuff. Nn.
Okay. Done.

Right, let me see what's there. Okay. Uh-huh. Mm. Right. I see.

What? What's there?

Looks like we're the prisoners of some ice golems. Probably taking us straight to the main baddy. Exciting!

Exciting? EXCITING? Aw! Why did I join Squirmin? If only I'd gone to Whifflewaff.

I say, ice golem. I have a special message for your boss. He'll be very interested to hear what I have to say.

Are you mad?

Think about it, Peck. We may as well be on the winning side.

Fair enough.

End recording.

CHAPTER 33

Louis felt like a total fool. Everything had been going so well. He'd done his ice training at school. They'd hidden from the storm and been fortunate with the goblins. They'd found some amazing costumes. But now their luck had run out. Somehow, his great friend Pearlin had become a baddy.

They were marched towards the entrance to the ice mine. It wasn't a nice, happy, welcoming entrance.

It was awful to see how mean Pearlin had become.

'All right. Everyone in,' she crowed. 'Find somewhere nice and cold to sit. Ha ha ha!'

They marched on down some icy steps and into an enormous ice cave. Louis looked around at the hundreds of people gathered there.

Catalogue sniffed the air and said, 'Eh! I recognise some of thems people over there.'

She pointed to a group of people sitting in a huddle and looking grumpy. It was the courtiers from Castle Sideways.

'There's King Burt the Not Bad,' said Louis, spotting the miserable monarch.

'That's not alls,' said Catalogue still sniffing, and pointing to a couple sitting on a big rock. It was Champion Trixie and Ned.

Louis gasped. 'Oh no! Mum and Dad!'

He waved at them, but they just looked confused.

'Of course!' thought Louis. 'I'm dressed up as a yeti!'

When they made it to the bottom of the steps, Pearlin made an announcement.

'Right, you lot, here's how it's going to go. I've designed this dastardly machine ... the world's biggest ice machine. You're going to build it. And then you're going to run round inside this big hamster wheel to make it work. We're going to turn the whole world into a ball of ice!'

Beside him, Yuki quivered with rage.

'Not again,' she squeaked, about to blow.

'Try not to shout, Yuki,' whispered Louis. 'You'll give us away.'

Somehow Yuki kept a lid on her temper. She said to herself, very quietly, 'Dragonflap, ho!'

Louis saw his mother raise a hand.

'What happens if we refuse to help?' Champion Trixie asked.

Pearlin pulled out her wand and fired off a blast of magic.

Trixie pushed Ned out of the way and dived for cover. The magic struck the rock they'd been sitting on and turned it into an enormous ice cube.

'Does that answer your question?' said Pearlin. 'Now, let's get started!'

'Come on,' Louis whispered to his friends. 'Let's get closer to Mum. If she's been here a while, she might already have a plan to get out!'

CHAPTER 34

Pearlin organised the prisoners into teams and got them working on her Blizzo Blaster straight away.

Louis managed to weave his way down to his mother.

'Psssst!' said Louis when he reached her.

'And the same to you,' said Trixie.

'Mum! It's me. Louis!'

'Louis! My poppet. At last!

PSSSST!

AND THE SAME TO YOU.

I knew you'd turn up sooner or later,' said Trixie with a smile in her voice.

'How long have you been here?' asked Louis.

'Long enough to put a spanner in the works of his last machine,' said Trixie with a chuckle. 'You should have seen it fall to pieces. Most impressive. And we'll do the same with this new one.'

'It won't be easy,' said Louis. 'Not if Pearlin is making it. She's a great inventor. And she's a wizard. A wizentor.'

'True. Poor Pearlin turned bad. It's awful,' said Trixie.

'I need to get out of here and face Splint. It's the only way to end this,' said Louis.

'Well, there's only two ways out,' said Trixie. 'And you'll never get out the main entrance. Too many ice golems.'

'What's the other way?'

She pointed upwards.

Louis looked to the roof of the ice mine. There was a hole in the ceiling. It looked familiar.

'That's where the machine puffs out the storm,' explained Trixie. 'Sends it up into the sky and off it goes.'

Where had Louis seen that shape before? Catalogue the penguin waddled over.

'Have you seen that hole?' she said. 'I reckon that hole leads up to that big daisy wotsit we saw. You knows, the thing next to the Great Lodge.'

'Right! So, that's what it's for,' said Louis.

'If you do get into the lodge, you'll have to watch out for Splint's little siblings too,' said Trixie. 'Five of the blighters. Hint. Flint. Mint. Clint and another one.'

'She's not called Sharon, is she?' asked Louis, remembering what Pearlin had said.

'That's her. Though I'm not sure she's as cold as the rest.'

'So how's you going to get up theres?' said Catalogue, looking at the hole far above them.

'I suppose you could fly Clunkie up there,' said Trixie, who'd quickly figured out who the woolly rhino was, 'but if Pearlin sees you, we'll be in big trouble.'

'Then we'll have to find another way out,' said Louis. He looked across at Yuki and said with a smile, 'We'll need to do some schoolwork.'

'Eh?' said Trixie and Catalogue.

But Yuki understood. 'Too right. Some A-grade ice climbing!'

CHAPTER 35

Above, in the Great Lodge, Crayko Le Faux was shaken out of the ice golem's bag. He landed with a thump on the ground in the meeting hall.

SWOOSH

BIFF! BASH!

Peck landed on top of him.

They looked up to see a very large snowball and a carrot.

'What are these things doing here?' said Splint, unimpressed.

'The ice golems found them out by Mount Sawtooth, your bossiness,' said Crunch. 'They said they had a special reason to see you, so I brought them right here!'

'Crunch, you fool,' said Splint. 'If we believed everyone who said they had a special reason to see me—'

Crayko dared to interrupt before it was too late. 'Please, your splendid snowness, we are here to help.'

'Yes, grovel, grovel,' said Peck, 'please don't freeze my circuits.'

'Oh fine, get on with it then,' said Splint, 'though it had better be good, or you'll be off to the ice mine.'

'Oh, it is good, oh great icy one,' said Crayko smarmily.

'Well? Out with it,' said Splint.

'What if I was to tell you that an army of knights from the future were going to launch an attack on Brrrrrland?' said Crayko.

'I'd say . . . I'd like to hear more about that,' said Splint, looking interested.

'And if I said I could help you defeat them, what would you say to that?' continued Crayko.

'I'd say that I'm suddenly looking for a champion knight,' said Splint. The sinister snowball recognised another cunning fellow when he saw one. 'I think you and your bird will fit in here nicely.'

Crayko smiled nastily and bowed deeply to his new master.

Nearby the other snowballs were watching on.

WELCOME TO THE TEAM.

SHOULD FIT IN HERE NICELY.

YOU'RE RIGHT ABOUT THAT COS HE'S HERE TO BETRAY HIS FRIENDS.

SHUT UP, SHARON!

CHAPTER NOT VERY LONG

Far away on the slopes of Mount Badaboom, Sir Tymur Trafela was pacing about in front of Dr Kyoob.

'Why haven't we heard from them?' he said anxiously.

'My calculations BEEP,' replied Dr Kyoob, 'are that DARP they have been captured or lost or both PORP.'

'Well, then, it's down to us,' said Sir Tymur. 'Tell the pupils we leave in an hour! This is our last chance to save the future! Oh dear!'

OH NO!
THEY'RE HEADING STRAIGHT
INTO CRAYKO'S TRAP!

CHAPTER
ALSO NOT VERY LONG

Deep inside Mount Sawtooth, Mac n Cheese had finished lighting the goblins' candles. The whole place shone with a cosy, yellow light. The goblins were thrilled.

'At last,' said Yob, 'we can finally see all the lovely things we've dropped in the dark.'

'Oh yes,' said Shob, 'there's my armour!'

'And there's my ice axe,' said Vob.

'And there's my preciousssssss,' said Mob.

'Your preciousssss?' quizzed Zob.

'Yessss. Ssss-sorry,' said Mob, 'going to sssss-sneeze! ATCHOO!'

'Bless you,' said Shob.

'As I was saying,' said Mob, 'there's my *precious* ring of invisibility.'

'Oo! Does it really work?' asked Yob.

'Course not,' said Mob. 'It's a joke one. From Ludmila's dress up shop. Remember.'

'Oh yes.'

The goblins did like to talk a lot, thought Mac n Cheese. They liked the goblins but were bored by all their chatter. What if Louis needed them?

Mac n Cheese turned and headed back to the cave entrance. They wished Pearlin was there. They really missed her.

CHAPTER 36

Pearlin's Blizzo Blaster, the terrible blizzard machine, was coming together fast. All the prisoners worked on it, including Louis and his friends. They were lifting, carrying, bolting and making.

But it wasn't the only thing being made. Louis was also making . . . a plan! A plan so hot it could have melted an iceberg. A plan to win the day.

'Here's what we know,' said Louis. 'Splint is indestructible. He's a snowball that can't be destroyed by magic. And he has lots of ice golems protecting him. We also know he never comes out of his lodge. So we need to find a way to get him out in the open. Then we might stand a chance of defeating him. We could biff him off to somewhere far away. Somewhere where he can't do any harm.'

'Yeah, but where's that funky place gonna be?' wondered Catalogue. 'And how we going to biff such a great big chilly billy?'

'I have an idea,' said Louis. 'If this Blizzo Blaster blizzard is as powerful as Pearlin says it will be, and if it shoots out of that hole up there . . . imagine what would happen if Splint was sitting on top of it?'

'It'd be WHOOSH O'CLOCK!' said Catalogue with glee.

'I like the sound of that,' said Trixie. 'But how will you draw him out?'

'Yuki and I will have to find a way. We'll sneak out of here and into the lodge. Time to put our ice climbing skills to the test.'

'Can't wait,' said Yuki. She was about to shout, 'DRAGONFLAP, HO!' But she stopped herself just in time and whispered it instead. 'Dragonflap, ho!'

'What is I supposed to be doing?' asked Catalogue. 'I don't want to be a spectator for all the fun times.'

'Nor me,' said Trixie.

'Do you still have those hot spicy plants?' asked Louis. (See Chapter 22 for details!)

'I doey,' said Catalogue. 'They're hiding inside me penguin outfit.'

'You're going to need them,' said Louis. And he outlined the rest of his plan to his friends. Last of all, he spoke to Clunkalot.

'Clunkie, once the Blizzo Blaster is almost ready, you fly right out of that hole in the ceiling. Find Mac n Cheese, then prepare to make a nuisance of yourselves. If things go to plan, there'll be hordes of ice golems that need steaming.'

'What are you lot talking about?' said a cool spiky voice.

It was Pearlin.

'Hurry up over there,' she barked. 'More work, less chat.'

She looked at Trixie and squinted at her, remembering. 'You. You're Knight Sir Louis' mother, aren't you? Where is he? If I know Louis, he'll be planning to save the world.'

'How should I know?' fibbed Trixie. 'I've been stuck here. But I do hope he comes. And I hope he finds a way to turn you into a good and proper wizentor again.'

'No chance,' said Pearlin. 'Never felt better. Or as powerful. When that little snowball blew an ice crystal up my nose and into my heart, it was the best day ever. This cold heart means I can get what I want, without having to worry about keeping any one else happy. Yeah.'

She walked off, laughing icily.

'So that's what happened,' said Louis to his mum. 'I'm sure you told me a bedtime story about that.'

'Yes, does seem familiar,' said Trixie. 'Anyway, we need to add it to the list. Cure Pearlin's heart.'

'Let's get started,' said Catalogue. 'This shopping list for saving the world is getting massive.'

CHAPTER 37

By the end of the day, the Blizzo Blaster was almost done. One more morning and it would be ready. The prisoners all found a corner to sleep in. Even Pearlin conked out. She slept while the ice golems stood guard.

In a dark corner, two yetis were sleeping. Or appeared to be. There was a quiet unzipping sound. From inside the two yeti costumes, Knight Sir Louis and Knight Sir Yuki stepped out. Then, carefully and quietly, they made the climb up, up, up the ice wall and towards the hole in the ceiling of the ice mine.

Trixie, Clunkie and Catalogue were watching from below, with fingers crossed (and trotters and hooves).

Everything was going smoothly until Louis reached for a piece of ice. It was loose. It broke free in his hand. The chunk flew through the air. It smashed onto the floor below with a THUMP and a KSSHHHHH. The ice golems turned to look with narrowing eyes. What was that?

Yuki and Louis stopped their climb. They stayed as still as they could. Pearlin was still asleep. But the golems were searching. Meanwhile, Clunkalot did some quick calculations. He could see the nearest ice golem walking towards the fallen ice. Surely, it would look up once it got there. It would see Louis. The whole plan would be over before it had been set in motion. There was nothing else for it. It was time for Clunkie to deploy his latest upgrade once again.

Clunkalot, still in his woolly rhino disguise, lifted his tail and let out a stink.

The smell.

What a smell!

No one had ever smelled a whiff that bad before.

A moment later everyone in the ice mine was awake, spluttering, coughing and running around desperate to find some fresh air.

Suddenly, the ice golems didn't know which

way to look. It was chaos. They forgot their search for the fallen ice. The stink woke Pearlin too. In the back of her clouded mind she thought, 'Wow, that smells just like that stink I installed in Clunkalot.'

Far above, Louis and Yuki breathed a sigh of relief. (The air up there was still fresh.)

'Nice one, Clunkie,' thought Louis to himself.

And they continued their climb towards the hole.

CHAPTER 38

In the lodge, Crayko was giving Splint and the mini snowballs a lecture on how to defeat the Knights of the Future School.

'They'll come the same way I did,' explained Crayko, 'over Mount Sawtooth.'

Crunch wasn't taking it very seriously.

WE'LL JUST LET THEM COME TO US HERE. WHAT HARM CAN A BUNCH OF SCHOOL KIDS DO? HA! WE'LL SEND THEM STRAIGHT TO THE ICE MINE.

'You're forgetting they are from the future,' said Crayko silkily.

'Yes, the future,' agreed Splint. 'A future where I have won. I'm not about to risk that, Crunch.'

Crunch sagged like a carrot left for too long in the fridge.

'Exactly, your icicle-ness,' said Crayko to Splint. 'They've grown up in an icy world. They know how to fight in the snow.'

'And they have Dr Kyoob,' said Peck.

'Dr Kyoob? Who's that?' said Splint. 'I hope he's not cube-shaped?'

'Oh, he is,' confirmed Crayko.

'Cubes! My least favourite shape,' said the spherical Splint. 'What's so special about this Kyoob?'

'He's a super amazing future robot wizard,' explained Crayko. 'He's dangerous. You can't let him anywhere near the lodge.'

'Yeah,' agreed Peck. 'And he says things like BEEP and DARP and BOOP. Don't know why, but it gives me the collywobbles.'

Splint didn't like the sound of this Dr Kyoob. Or collywobbles. Or these future children. These brats were a menace to *his* future.

'Very well,' said Splint. 'I will order my ice golems to march out and meet them.'

'How many shall we send?' asked Prime Minister Crunch. 'One? Two?'

'All of them. All but the five in the ice mine,' said Splint. 'Get the job done.'

Crunch ran off to carry out her orders.

'What about you, my supreme overlord?' asked Crayko. 'Will you go too? Lead the fight?'

'Of course not,' said Splint. 'I never leave my lodge. My snowball siblings will stay too. And Iggy my ice golem. And you, Crayko. You and your bird will defend the lodge if your schoolmates make it this far.'

'Absolutely, my supreme overlord,' said Crayko, bowing deeply.

'Stay indoors? Away from the fight?' said Peck. 'Sounds good. Nice one.'

CHAPTER 39

Splint rolled off his leather chair and away to his private study.

Crayko smiled to himself. Things were going well. Splint seemed to be impressed by him.

'It won't last, you know,' said a voice.

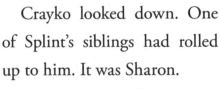

Crayko looked down. One of Splint's siblings had rolled up to him. It was Sharon.

'I've seen it before. Some useful person turns up. Splint uses them for a bit. Then he starts to get suspicious.

He won't trust you for long. Soon, he'll be convinced you're here to betray him. Then he'll arrange a nice holiday for you . . . to a bottomless pit. He's like that. Doesn't trust anyone, really. Terrible person to be a leader, if you think about it.'

'Good point, that,' said Peck.

'Shhhh!' said Mint, who was rolling up beside his sister. 'Sharon! Shut up! Do you want Splint to hear you?'

Sharon scoffed, 'What's he going to do? Freeze me?'

Crayko shrugged. 'What you say may be true. But I will stay loyal to Splint, no matter what. I will show him that he can trust me. Now, if you'll excuse me, I must prepare.'

And Crayko turned on his heels and strode away.

'They're all the same,' said Sharon, yawning and heading for her snow-bed. 'Power mad. Why can't people just be nice to each other?'

'Don't be ridiculous,' said Mint, rolling alongside her.

'Would you like me to cuddle you or kick you?'
asked Sharon.

'Hmm. Cuddle, I suppose,' said Mint.

'There you go then,' said Sharon. 'Even you
prefer nice, really.'

'Oh. Yeah,' said
Mint, confused.
'Hadn't
thought about
it like that.'

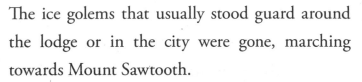

Soon the palace was
quiet and seemed empty.
The ice golems that usually stood guard around
the lodge or in the city were gone, marching
towards Mount Sawtooth.

The battle of Brrrrrland was about to begin.

DUN DUN DURRRRRRR

CHAPTER 40

Sir Tymur Trafela, Dr Kyoob and the students of KOFS were heading towards Mount Sawtooth. They flew in on all kinds of flying machines.

'Forward, brave students!' called Sir Tymur. 'Don't forget to take notes. You'll all be writing an essay on it afterwards.'

'Hopefully, BOOP,' said Dr Kyoob, 'the essays will be titled DARP *How We Saved The Future* BEEP.'

And on they sped to battle!

ALSO...
DUN DUN
DURRRRRRR

CHAPTER 41

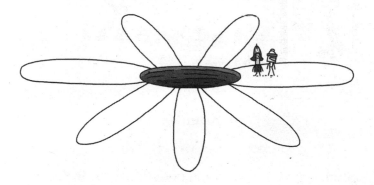

As dawn broke, Louis and Yuki finally made it out of the hole in the roof.

Flashes of light in the distance caught their eye. As he stood at the top of the ice mine, Louis could see ice golems marching out of the city and up the mountain. Somewhere near the back of the line was a very miserable-looking carrot.

'Wonder where they're going?' said Yuki.

'Wherever it is, it's good luck for us,' said Louis. 'Should be a lot easier to slip inside the lodge now.'

Before they crept away, they looked back down inside the ice mine. Pearlin was already working the prisoners hard.

'Not long before the Blizzo Blaster's ready,' said Louis. 'We don't have much time.'

They crept over to the lodge. Louis pulled Dave from his scabbard.

'Time to chop some wood, I think,' said Louis and he cut a hole in the wooden beams. It was easy work for Dave. His blade was sharper than a sharp thing that's been sharpened with a sharpener. Louis and Yuki crawled inside and found themselves in a tiny bedroom. A bedroom for five tiny snowballs!

Uh-oh!

Quick as a flash Yuki pulled off her cape and turned it into a makeshift bag.

Louis grabbed Flint, Mint, Hint, Clint and Sharon and threw them inside.

'That's five little problems in the bag,' said Louis with a smile.

ARR GRR NNN URG OO! VELVETY.

Louis and Yuki soon found their way to the large meeting hall.

'How are we going to lure Splint out of the lodge?' asked Yuki.

Louis wasn't sure. But as he looked around at the deserted room, he made a decision. 'Do you know what?' he said. 'I'm fed up of all this sneaking about. It's not very Dragonflap, is it?'

'Not really, no,' said Yuki.

'I think it's time we stopped hiding in the shadows and faced Splint. Yuki, use that impressive voice of yours.'

'A pleasure,' said Yuki. She took a deep breath and shouted:

OI! SPLINT! DRAGONFLAP, HO!

The room echoed and shuddered with the noise. Then all fell silent.

Finally, a rolling, grinding sound started up and four figures appeared in the meeting hall to face them.

Peck.

Crayko Le Faux.

Iggy the Ice Golem.

And Splint, Supreme Overlord of Brrrrland, the Sinister Snowball.

CHAPTER 42

Down in the ice mine, Pearlin was smiling. It wasn't her old cheery smile with a friendly twinkle in her eyes. It was a smile of teeth and staring, cruel eyes. She was thrilled because, at last, the Blizzo Blaster was . . .

READY? IS IT READY? I THINK IT'S READY.

'IT'S READY!' announced Pearlin.

'It's true. It's ready,' said Trixie to Catalogue, worried.

'Here's hoping Louis is also ready steady go,' said Catalogue, before turning to the woolly rhino beside her. 'Right, Clunkie, it's time to fly. Go get Mac n Cheese. The final battle is brewing and something tells me a dragon with two fiery noggins is gonna be a good thing to have around.'

Clunkie didn't need to be asked twice. He unfurled his wings and leapt into the air.

Flying woolly rhinoceroses tend to attract a lot of attention.

The ice golems started hurling bolts of ice at Clunkie. Pearlin screamed at them to stop.

'FOOLS! You'll hit the Blizzo Blaster! I'll deal with this . . .'

And Pearlin pulled a magic wand from her clothes. She prepared to zap Clunkie out of the air.

Trixie wasn't about to let that happen. She ran, jumped and slid across the ice, bumping into Pearlin. Pearlin's bolt of magic blasted out of her wand, but in totally the wrong direction. It ping-ponged around the ice mine walls until it zapped into an ice golem which exploded into snowflakes.

'Oo!' said Catalogue. 'Quite a pretty way to go BOOM.'

Meanwhile, Clunkie shed his woolly rhino disguise which fell down on top of Pearlin.

'Agh! Get this off me! Get it off!' came her muffled cries.

Two ice golems lifted it away. Pearlin looked up, but the flying animal was gone.

'What was that?' she barked at Trixie.

'Why are you always asking me?' said Trixie, being tricksy. 'I don't know anything.'

Pearlin was furious. But then she remembered the Blizzo Blaster. Her smile returned and she pointed to the giant wheel they'd made, large enough to fit forty or fifty people inside.

'It doesn't matter what it was,' said Pearlin, 'because you and your fellow prisoners are about to power my greatest invention ever! GET IN!'

Trixie, Catalogue and a bunch of the other prisoners were pushed forward.

'Let's not get this moving too quickly,' whispered Trixie. 'We have to give Louis time to lure Splint out.'

'No problemo,' said Catalogue. 'We'll says we're doing a practice. In the meantimes, I'll hand out some spicy wotsits to get us going super-fast later.'

Just then, poor King Burt stepped up towards Pearlin. He looked very sorry for himself.

'I can't do this,' he said. 'Pearlin. Don't you remember me? Old kingy wingy. We're chums.'

'I remember you making me dance like a clown,' said Pearlin. 'Get on!'

'Oh, poor me,' said Burt and was first to step aboard the wheel. When Pearlin had walked off towards the control lever, a penguin approached King Burt. It handed him some sort of vegetable.

'Here, your majestic wonder,' it said. 'Eat this magma root. It'll give a nice kick.'

'I don't accept gifts from strange penguins,' said the king.

The penguin pulled back her disguise. It was Catalogue, of course.

'Oh! I say,' said Burt. He managed a little smile. 'Is there hope?'

'Might be, your specialness,' said Catalogue. 'Now, take this hot rootle and pass these other fiery foodles to the rest of the wheel crew. Louis needs us to be running on full power. But don't eat it until I says gobble.'

'Oh dear!' said the king, munching. 'I'm afraid I've already had a bite. Terribly hungry, you see.'

'Uh-oh,' said Catalogue.

'Yes. Uh-oh,' said Burt, whose face was turning a violent shade of purple.

The root was hot.

It was very hot.

It was extremely, unpleasantly hot.

King Burt started to run like a motor!

'No,' said Trixie, 'it's too soon!'

CHAPTER 43

Back in the Great Lodge, Louis and Yuki stood facing Splint, Iggy and Crayko.

Yuki was quivering with rage.

'Crayko Le Faux! I can't believe that even you would stoop so low! To join forces with this silly snowball! ARRRRRR.'

But before she could explode, Louis spoke.

'It's okay, Yuki. Things aren't quite as bad as they seem. Are they, Crayko?'

SQUIRMIN HO!

'Right, Louis. Everything went just like you said it would.' And he shouted . . .

. . . before spinning on his heels and joining Yuki and Louis.

'Sorry, boss,' said Crayko to Splint. 'Wasn't really on your team at all. By the way, thanks for agreeing to send all your ice golems away. That's going to help us win. HA!'

Yuki still wasn't sure what was going on.

Neither was Peck. 'Can somebody tell me who I'm supposed to peck?'

Let's imagine for a moment that this book has a rewind button. Let's rewind to before Louis left the Knights of the Future School.

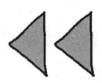

240

Now, let's fast forward back to the present moment. Press here!

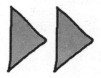

Yuki looked at Crayko in amazement. 'Does this mean we're on the same team?'

'Afraid so, Sir Yuki,' said Crayko with a grin. 'Squirmin and Dragonflap together. Who'd have thought it?'

Splint stayed very still. He looked at the three knights and bird opposite.

'You're all so very small,' he said, at last. 'You won't last long. Iggy! Get them!'

Iggy the Ice Golem was the most impressive of all the golems. He wielded a huge ice scythe and now he took it and swung it towards the three knights.

They jumped to safety just in time and drew their swords.

Louis fought sword to scythe with the giant, while Crayko and Yuki tried to chip away at his body, which was made from hard ice.

'He's solid,' shouted Crayko. 'He's invincible!'

'What you need is some sort of bird that is good at pecking,' said Peck, flying in.

He landed on Iggy's head and started pecking at it. He didn't really make a dent in the icy head. But the vibrations of his pecking made Iggy's body shudder and shake.

PECKITY PECKITY PECK

Iggy roared and reached up to swat away the bird. For a moment he was distracted. Louis saw his chance. There was a little nick in the ice scythe about halfway up. Louis swung Dave, aiming precisely at the nick. The scythe shattered into a million pieces.

SWOOSH

SMASH!

'Thanks, Peck!' said Louis. 'Keep going.'

Peck continued to fly and peck, fly and peck and Iggy twisted and turned trying to stop him. Iggy bumped into Splint's big leather chair, lost his balance, and fell backwards onto Splint himself. The only thing harder than Iggy the Ice Golem, was Splint the Sinister Snowball. Iggy exploded into snowflakes.

He was gone.

'Looks like it's just you and us now, Splint,' said Louis, before turning to the others and whispering.

'Get ready to run. We have to get him outside. Everything depends on it.'

Just then, there was a huge rumbling.

'What's that?' said Yuki.

'That,' said Splint with a nasty grin, 'is the sound of a Blizzo Blaster working. It is the sound of my victory. The sound of an eternal winter  storm. HA HA HA HA! I win. So there!'

From somewhere inside Yuki's sack of smaller snowballs, five voices could be heard.

GO SPLINT!

SPLINT FOREVER!

BIG BROTHER RULES!

SO SINISTER.

AW! I WAS LOOKING FORWARD TO HIM LOSING.

SHARON! SHUT UP!

CHAPTER 44

The Blizzo Blaster was working at top speed. King Burt had eaten his magma root and was now running like a rocket. The machine hissed and whirred. It jetted out a thin stream of freezing cold snow which flew out of the ice mine through the hole in the ceiling and up, up, up into the air.

As the blizzard rose higher it spread out in every direction. The blizzard raced towards the ring of mountains. It rushed over the peaks and down towards the countries below. The world-changing storm was on its way!

Sir Tymur and his knights had just flown into Brrrrrland when the storm hit. They crashed down onto the mountainside. Worse luck, they looked

up to find an army of ice golems approaching.
Strangely, there seemed to be a walking, talking
carrot leading the golems.

I CALCULATE BOOP DEEP THAT THERE ARE LURP TWICE AS MANY ICE GOLEMS AS US =BLARP=

Sir Tymur looked at Dr Kyoob, worried. Things were going very badly for them. Then his expression changed. He looked determined. He reached for his helmet and put it on.

'Knights of the Future School,' shouted Sir Tymur. 'The time for battle is here. I will be giving marks for this battle. Who wants an A star?'

The knights roared and raced down through the blizzard to fight the golems.

CHAPTER FAILURE.

Louis, Yuki and Crayko watched the blizzard from inside the lodge in total dismay.

'It won't be long,' said Splint, 'until the whole world is covered in a blanket of beautiful snow. And I will be supreme overlord of the whole world!'

'No!' said Yuki. 'Not again.'

'You're too nasty, even for Squirmin house,' said Crayko, in despair.

'We can't have lost,' said Yuki. 'No no no!'

Just then Yuki's makeshift bag split open and the snowballs leapt out. Louis watched Clint, Mint, Flint and Hint roll over to their big brother. Splint smiled and laughed with glee.

'Yes,' said Splint with a huge smile, 'you have failed!'

CHAPTER 45

Down in the ice mine, King Burt finally ran out of steam. He collapsed onto the wheel and the Blizzo Blaster slowed.

'We need to stop anyone else getting on the Blizzo Blaster,' said Trixie. 'Let's buy Louis some time.'

'I got an idea,' said Catalogue and she walked up to Pearlin. 'Oi! Evilly Pearlin! Guess who's come to tea?'

Pearlin turned to look at the strange penguin walking towards her. Catalogue unzipped her penguin outfit and stepped out.

'I is returned to end your whopping great big plans of making the world a snow doughnut,' announced the brave boar.

Pearlin looked across at her former friend and narrowed her eyes.

'So, it was you all along, Catalogue,' said Pearlin. 'Pfft! You turning up here changes nothing. In fact, you can go on the wheel next.'

'I wills,' agreed Catalogue, 'but first I want to be telling you about Mac n Cheese. They is missing you something rotten.'

Pearlin stopped still. The mention of her old pet Mac n Cheese touched her cold heart. It beat a little faster for a moment.

'Where are they?' asked Pearlin, a quiver in her voice.

Trixie smiled beneath her helmet. It was working. Pearlin was distracted.

The wheel that powered the Blizzo Blaster completely stopped and King Burt rolled off. Far above, the blaster stopped spewing out snow and ice. Trixie hoped Louis would find a way of getting Splint out of his lodge. It was probably their last chance for victory.

CHAPTER 46

Just in case you're wondering how the battle's going between Sir Tymur's knights and the ice golems . . . here's a quick update from the Dark Ages News Team with Lady Shufflepaper and Squire Chattymouth.

NEWS FLASH

—DARK AGES NEWS—

DUM BONG DUM BONG
BING A LING A LING

Hello. And this just in . . .

The Blizzo Blaster blizzard has vanished.

Reports suggest the Knights of the Future School have been joined by hordes of mountain goblins, a robot horse with wings and a double-headed dragon.

Ice golems are being blasted into snowflakes everywhere.

Reports say Prime Minister Crunch was last seen hiding behind a rock saying, 'Uh oh!'

CHAPTER 47

Louis, Yuki and Crayko looked at Splint and his sibling snowballs. There seemed to be no way to get Splint out of his lodge.

Louis' planning brain was throwing out ideas.

WHAT ABOUT...

... USING DAVE TO BRING A BUNCH OF WALRUSES HERE? THEY COULD BUMP SPLINT OUT?

... BLOWING REALLY HARD TO SEE IF HE'LL ROLL?

... TELLING HIM HE SMELLS BAD AND HOPING HE'LL TAKE A REALLY HOT, MELTY SHOWER?

... JUMPING ON TOP OF HIM AND ROLLING HIM OUT?

That last idea wasn't too bad, thought Louis, but Splint interrupted his planning.

'Nothing can stand between me and my future,' said Splint. 'I win.'

His siblings agreed.

'Yeah,' said Clint.

'Right,' said Hint.

'Ha ha!' said Flint.

'Hmm. Suppose,' said Mint, who was having a change of heart after Sharon had offered him a cuddle earlier.

'You see, all my siblings agree,' said Splint. 'They may not be as smart as me, but they know what's good for them.'

'Wait a minute,' said Louis. 'You're missing someone.'

He was right. One of the snowballs hadn't come out of the bag to join the others. She showed

 her face now. It was Sharon. She jumped out of the bag.

'If you're so smart, big brother,' she said to Splint, 'how come you can't even count up to five. All of your siblings do not agree.'

'You were always my least favourite,' said Splint cruelly.

Sharon bounced up onto Louis' shoulder.

She whispered in his ear. 'Here's a fun fact. Splint is hollow. Goodness knows what would happen if someone got inside him.'

Louis looked at Crayko and Yuki. They had the same idea. As one, they ran towards Splint.

Splint roared.

'FOOOOOLLLS.'

This meant he had to open his mouth very wide.

Louis, Crayko and Yuki leapt into the air . . .

. . . in a beautiful arc . . .

. . . and landed PLOP! . . .

. . . inside the Sinister Snowball.

'Here we go, everyone,' said Louis. 'Time to drive this ball out of here!'

CHAPTER 48

Louis and his chums drove Splint out of the meeting hall, down the hallway and crashed through the front doors of the lodge. Then they changed direction, heading straight for the ice mine hole.

But just before they reached it, the four smaller snowballs wedged themselves in front of Splint and he suddenly stopped rolling. Louis and the others were thrown out of his mouth and onto the snow.

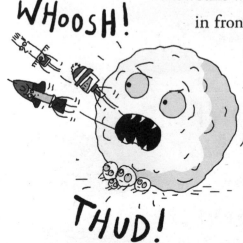

WHOOSH!

THUD!

'You'll spend the rest of your days in the ice mine!' spluttered Splint, fuming.

Louis saw how close Splint was to the hole. So close, and yet so far. Then, he looked up at the lodge behind them all and another idea popped into his head. The roof was stacked with snow, including a fresh layer from the latest blizzard.

'Yuki,' he said, 'sorry about this, but I'm going to make you a little bit angry.'

'What?' said Yuki, confused.

'You see,' said Louis, 'I think Squirmin house is better than Dragonflap.'

Yuki was outraged. She opened her mouth and said,

HOW DARE YOU, LOUIS! DRAGONFLAP IS THE BEST FOREVER! DRAGONFLAP HOOOOOO!

The astonishing noise of Yuki's voice wobbled the whole lodge. The snow on the roof shuddered, then slid like an avalanche towards them all.

'RUN FOR COVER!' said Louis.

Crayko, Yuki, Peck, Sharon and Louis dived out of the way. But Splint was still wedged where he was by the other four snowballs. The avalanche hit him and biffed him into the ice mine hole.

'OI!' shouted Splint. 'GET ME OUT OF HERE!'

'Don't worry,' said Louis, 'that's just what we're planning.'

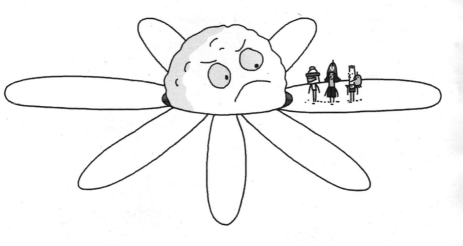

CHAPTER 49

In the ice mine below, Catalogue was still keeping Pearlin busy with talk of Mac n Cheese. Suddenly it went dark. Trixie looked up and saw Splint roll into the hole above them.

She shouted, 'It's now or never!'

Everyone jumped onto the Blizzo Blaster wheel as one and chomped down on their hot roots and glowing mushrooms.

'Soz, Pearlin, gotta go runnin' now,' said Catalogue and she joined the others.

Pearlin had no idea what was going on. Why did everyone suddenly want to work the Blizzo Blaster?

The ice mine prisoners started to run. And wow, could they run fast!

The Blizzo Blaster was working once more. And this time it was at maximum power!

PoFFFF!

CHAPTER 50

Splint was desperatcly trying to roll himself out of his hole, but it was no good. Three of his loyal siblings jumped inside his mouth to try and roll him out the way Louis had. But that didn't help.

Meanwhile Mint had decided he'd rather stick with Sharon.

Louis heard the sound of the Blizzo Blaster firing up. 'Well, Supreme Overlord, it wasn't very nice meeting you. Goodbye. Have a good trip.'

'WHAAT?' screamed Splint.

A moment later the blizzard shot towards him and blasted Splint up on top of it . . . up . . . up . . . up . . . higher than anyone else in history! (Well, except for Clunkalot.)

And now the final score.

FINAL SCORE

KNIGHT SIR LOUIS **1** | **0** SPLINT THE SINISTER SNOWBALL

HOORAH!

CHAPTER 51.

As Splint made his journey into orbit, Louis heard the clatter of armour. He turned to see the goblins approaching with Sir Tymur, Dr Kyoob and the KOFS.

They'd defeated the ice golems. Hoorah!

Prime Minister Crunch was led forward in irons.

'I was only doing what I was told,' said Crunch, using the worst excuse ever in the history of the universe.

'It's all over,' said Sir Tymur.

'Not quite yet,' said Louis, looking at the blizzard still blasting into the air. 'There's still one more person we need to save.'

Louis looked up and saw Clunkalot and Mac n Cheese flying in. Louis ran towards them and jumped onto Clunkie's back.

'Come on! Time to see an old friend!' said Louis.

And they flew into the entrance of the ice mine.

The last four ice golems stood in their way, but Mac n Cheese's fiery breath soon turned them into piles of snow.

At the sight of Louis, Champion Trixie roared to the other prisoners, 'Everybody! Stop running! Stop it now!'

They stopped pedalling and the Blizzo Blaster ground to a halt.

Pearlin shouted with fury, 'What are you all doing? Get back to work!'

'Pearlin!' shouted Louis. 'That's enough!'

She turned on him, the blue glow strong in her narrowed eyes, 'And who's going to stop me? Not you!'

She raised her wand. Louis spoke fast before she could cast a spell.

'Wait! I've brought someone to see you,' said Louis and he pointed to Mac n Cheese. They glided down from above, softly and slowly.

Pearlin raised her wand as if to strike, but then hesitated, and lowered her wand.

'Mac n Cheese,' she muttered.

The double-headed dragon came into land beside her with hardly a sound. The dragon wrapped itself around her in a monster-sized cuddle.

'Aw!' said Catalogue who was watching from the Blizzo Blaster. 'That's a loverrly old sight right there.'

It was just as Louis had hoped. Mac n Cheese's dragon cuddle was warmed with dragon fire. The warmth went straight to Pearlin's cold heart and melted the shard of ice that had poisoned it. A moment later, her heart beat faster, her eyes turned to their usual brown and Pearlin was her old self!

'Cor, that was awful,' said Pearlin, giving each dragon head a big kiss. 'I went badder than a slice of ham in the sunshine!'

Louis, Catalogue, Trixie and even King Burt joined Mac n Cheese in the biggest hug of their friend, Pearlin. Louis saw Sir Tymur coming down to see what was going on.

'Now it's over,' shouted Louis to the headmaster.

'Very good, Sir Louis,' said Sir Tymur. 'I'm giving you an A plus plus plus plus for saving the world!'

CHAPTER

FIFTY STUFF

Let's just wrap up a few loose ends.

Louis

Louis and his friends went back home to Castle Sideways. King Burt gave everyone their old jobs back. They celebrated as always with a fine banquet. King Burt had beans on toast.

The Splong

Mysto and the other frozen wizards were freed by Pearlin. She popped back to Fuming Wood and Mac n Cheese helped to thaw them out using some low-level dragon snorts. Mysto apologised for buying his ice from a suspicious carrot.

Knights of the Future School

Inspired by their win, Sir Tymur and the KOFS decided to do some more time travelling and see if they could find others in need of their skills. Crayko Le Faux and Yuki became great friends! Dragonflap, ho! Squirmin, ho!

Peck finally accepted that he was a woodpecker and was given his own tree to peck and live inside.

Brrrrrland

Brrrrrland had a proper vote and installed a new leader . . . Sharon. She decided to end Splint's eternal winter. She let the weather do what it wanted. Brrrrrland still had four seasons of winter, but they were slightly different.

Crunch

Prime Minister Crunch was imprisoned under the mountain with the goblins. She discovered she quite liked it there, especially if they turned out the lights. Carrots really do like being underground in the dark.

Splint and the Snowballs

And Splint? Splint just went round and round and round and round the planet with his three little siblings.

Acknowledgements

Thank you to Sir Bella Pearson for your guidance, wisdom and belief. Thank you for guiding these stories away from the Bogs of Wattasmel and towards the heights of Mount Badaboom.

Thank you to Sir Gaia Banks, Sir Lucy Fawcett, Sir Colyn Allsopp, Sir Liz Scott, Sir Ness Wood and Sir Hannah Featherstone.

Thank you to Evgenia and Lucy for your love and support.

And thank you to Louis, now all grown up, for being the original audience of one.

Have you read the other stories about Knight Sir Louis?

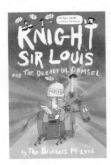   

'Sublime daftness on every page!' Jeremy Strong

Knight Sir Louis is the champion knight at Castle Sideways, and the bravest of all knights in all lands. Braver than Knight Sir Colin in the bogs of Wattasmel. Braver than Knight Sir Barbara in the mountains of Itso-Hy. Even braver than Knight Sir Gary from the soggy lands of Tippinitdown.

But Louis is modest. He says he's not brave, but just good at staying calm when everyone else is going completely bonkers.

Along with his trusty mechanical steed, Clunkalot, and mystical sword, Dave, Knight Sir Louis and his friends are sent to do battle with the Damsel of Distresse who is terrorising the land, stealing coins of gold, silver and chocolate. But soon he finds himself dealing with strong enchantments, powerful magic, and evil potatoes . . . all in a normal day for this brave knight. (Just don't mention wasps.) Hooray for Knight Sir Louis!

'A masterclass in silliness!' Gary Northfield